CASTING OUT SECRETS

THE WITCH OF HENBANE ISLAND
BOOK 3

POPPY BRIDGEMAN

Ebook ISBN: 978-1-990509-41-4
Paperback ISBN: 978-1-990509-42-1
Audio book ISBN:978-1-990509–43-8

Cover created by Getcovers

FREE BOOK

Claim your copy of Magic Will Out when you sign up for my newsletter and follow Cossi as she seeks answers to her past. Use the QR code to claim your copy now.

1

I tucked my new bike into the last space on the rack in the bike park. She would be safe there from the casual bumps that would scrape and ding her pretty lilac paint. Yes, I knew it would happen, unless I intended to never ride her and simply display her on my wall. But keeping her pristine for as long as possible felt like I was treating her right.

D and I were on the mainland yesterday for our date. I got my bike — she would be named soon. I also picked up the fleece for paying the raccoon grandmother, although I kept most of it in case I needed her help again.

We ate lunch and took a long walk around the town and along the beach. No one was murdered, at least no magical person. It was a great first date all around.

The only shadow on the day was in my own head. In the week since we'd caught Greentree Boll, I carried the suspicion that the two murders were linked, and that someone was behind them. And that Mrs. Vestum was right; I might not be the reason people were dying, but it started the day I arrived.

I just needed to prove it, and that was the huge problem. How did you prove someone was convincing witches to murder witches without sounding like a conspiracy nut?

The wind from the ocean carried a bite when we took the boat back. It wasn't fall yet, but the evenings were getting cooler, and the days didn't scorch. I took a deep breath and patted the seat of my bike. Time to get to Jan's for my shift. Then I'd be free to figure out my next steps with building my new business.

"Beulah." I had no idea why I needed to say it out loud, but it was my bike's name. Maybe a magic thing. Oh, I very much hoped my elusive third power was talking to mechanical things.

By the time the day was over, I'd talked to Jan about builders, electricians, and plumbers, only to find out there were two people who took care of everything. One contractor and one electrician/plumber. It kind of made sense. There was only one doctor, one lawyer and one cop.

The next few days were going to be busy making arrangements. And I still needed to figure out my blocked third power, practice casting spells while I learned more of them, and learn how to run a business on an invisible magic island. One of those would be enough to fill my days, but all three were important. And if I'd grown up on Henbane, most of it would have been taken care of by the time I'd turned five.

I tossed my apron in the laundry basket and washed my hands. The cafe business was steady all day, giving both me and Jan enough to do. Now that my shift was over, there was only one table filled with earth witches. They had full beers, and their dinner plates were cleared.

"If you need help setting up The Inner Spell, just let me know," Jan said. "You'll get a list of tasks from the council, but there's nothing like experience to get you through the hoops."

Lilibeth offered the same when I told her the council approved my application. "I guess I should look to Phillip, too. He's my mentor, after all," I said. "Is there anyone around with recent experience? Not that I don't value your input, but it's been a long time since you went through the process."

"We have long memories," Jan said, "and this is Henbane; the process doesn't change. Phillip is a good resource even though he inherited the bookstore. He still had to be approved."

I assumed inheriting meant an easy approval. My assumptions turned out to be wrong every time, but it's hard to change every single thing about you and what you know. The only sure thing was the witches and shifters were just like humans. They could be petty, and murderous, and judgmental, and every other negative and positive characteristic of a living being.

"I'll ask him tonight," I said. "I need a day off from magic research, anyway."

"Not too many," Jan said. "There are a lot of everyday spells you need to master to run a business. And that third power is still inside you."

Yeah, yeah, I didn't have anything on my list that wasn't priority number one. "I won't forget any of it. Thanks for the names of the contractors. See you tomorrow."

THE BOOKSTORE WAS JUST CLOSING AS I got home. Five minutes to clean up, grab my laptop and notes and then I was sitting at the kitchen table, ready to work. A nice controllable to-do list with tasks I could tick off as done was just what I needed. I could work in my room, but if I wanted to talk to Phillip, I had to come out. The security spell bag was still in place, and it wasn't going anywhere until I could make one with more flexible controls.

"Have you eaten?" Phillip asked. He placed his ledgers on the other side of the table. Working like this was a habit we'd fallen into.

"At Jan's," I said. "I could make us some tea."

"I'll do it," he said. I heard the unvoiced 'because you are still not quite capable of it'.

I decided to ask for my favor while he made his sandwich, peanut butter and jam. Apparently being a really old witch didn't stop you eating like a kid.

"Can you work with me to get the business up and running?" I didn't want to be too specific, mainly because I had no real idea what I'd need.

"I'm your mentor, Cossi, that's what I do."

To be honest, I'd become suspicious of his role as I talked to other witches. When the subject of my training or integrating into Henbane society came up, a few people expressed surprise he hadn't told me or taught me something.

"I'm going to reach out to the contractor tomorrow," I said, because his tone didn't leave room for me to say thanks. "What else?"

"I think the best way is for you to shadow me as I run my business. That way I can answer specific questions, and you will learn on the job, so to speak."

"What about Lilibeth and Jan?"

"I'll speak to them. They can find other help," he said.

2
———

I convinced Phillip to let me start in the afternoon when we set up the next morning. He might have thought it was okay to dump Jan and Lilibeth in favor of full-time at the bookstore, but I wasn't going to let that just happen. Even if they didn't really need me, surely a bit of notice was just polite.

I dropped in to talk to Jan first, he didn't care. Or he didn't want me to feel bad. When I told him I'd be available if he really needed help, he said, "I'm surprised this didn't happen earlier. Phillip should be using up more of your time. I've been wondering how he's managing to teach you with everything else going on."

That wasn't the first comment about Phillip's performance as my mentor. I didn't know enough about what was expected to defend him, or me, or agree with them. I was constantly questioning my assumptions about Henbane, but that was me doing my usual second guessing.

Lance was back at the shifter village, but D agreed to meet at Lilibeth's pet store/daycare. So, I ordered three coffees to go and headed over to meet them.

"So, he's going to show you all about managing a business?" Lilibeth asked after I told them both the new plan.

"Not just that," I said automatically. Then I thought back, and really, that's what he'd said. "I'm sure some magic training will happen."

"You can't just let it happen casually," D said. "Spell training requires focus, and we still need to find that third power. There's a reason your parents blocked it."

"And being with him all day won't help you get to know more of the people on Henbane," Lilibeth said. "And what about Destroyer? Phillip won't be happy to have him in the store."

I covered my ears. Childish, I know, but I couldn't think. When I walked in to Run, Fly, Slither, I thought I had a good plan. Now I just couldn't think. Too many opinions. Too few answers.

When they stopped speaking, I uncovered my ears and grabbed my coffee, ready to bring some order to the conversation. Then Iris, an old lab mix, chimed in. "When will you practice talking to us?"

That was one power I thought I had perfected. "What practice do I need?"

I pointed to Iris when Lilibeth and D both stared at me like I'd lost my mind.

"You still shout. You don't know our names. Have you done any research into our behavior? We're not all the same, you know."

"Fine. Let's all agree I have too much on my plate," I said. "I've got some contractor meeting with me about The Inner Spell, so that will be less work. After I make the decisions, the building gets done. I'm not out there with a drill or anything. That's one thing dealt with."

"At least Phillip is helping you with the business," D

said. "We could all have chipped in, but having one person teaching you will make it faster. Fewer points of view getting in the way."

"And I can talk to animals on my breaks," I said. "I just need a list of things I'm doing wrong so I can practice."

"A list from every kind of animal," Iris said.

I chose to ignore the complication.

"Spell work I can practice as I need one," I said.

"You should follow the curriculum from our schools," Lilibeth said.

Like I was in first grade? Well, in this respect, I was. "Can I get that, so I have guidance?"

Lilibeth nodded and sent a text.

"Your third power?" D asked.

To be fair, he'd done most of the work with me to winkle it out. But that would have to go on the back burner. Until I had a lot more experience under my belt, all I would get out of constant failed tests was a headache.

"When I'm settled," I said. "It's blocked, and the earth witches think the block should be fading without my dad reinforcing it."

"But it hasn't," D said.

"As far as we know," I said. "I'm working on the assumption that the block was all about us living in the non-magical world. And the power might be unblocked but subtle."

He frowned as he thought that over. "Maybe. But you should know when you're using power."

"How?" I asked. "If there's some kind of feeling when I use power, I have no idea. When I read people's emotions, there's nothing to show I'm doing it other than I can read them. Like right now, you are both frustrated. Sorry, I try not to read you. Same when I talk to animals."

He mock-glared at me; it was clear it was an act by the grin that ruined the scowl. "I was thinking you'd see results, but I guess if it's subtle, you wouldn't know."

"I still think you need more flexibility," Lilibeth said. "Don't let Phillip monopolize you."

Did they think I'd let our friendship peter away? "I still plan on hanging out," I said, "and gossiping. Phillip doesn't control me. But he's offered to actually mentor me."

I didn't want this to be a thing between us. With less time to socialize, hanging out needed to be fun, not a chore to keep them in my life.

"You're right," D said, "and the council gave you Phillip, so they think he's the best fit. I'm sure if you ask, he'll get into the magic and power with you."

Lilibeth didn't appear convinced. "And if there's another crime?"

"I hope there isn't," I said, "but I'll figure it out. We can't break up the most successful detectives on the island."

She laughed. "Don't let Mark hear you say that."

I checked my watch. "Time for my first lessons."

3

The day with Phillip wasn't quite as boring as I expected. Yes, I got an advanced degree in stocking shelves with obscure books, but I also had my first experience of the reporting system. All the businesses on Henbane reported income and expenses through the same bookkeeping program. Ashely, the island's accountant, did all the work to reconcile and report. I hoped she had a magic power to help her, or better, help her clients, because the financial stuff was always a chore for me.

We were sitting at the cash desk having a tea break and generally talking about business when my mind started nagging me about the mentorship thing. What exactly did it entail? Was Phillip doing a good job or a bad job? Was it my place to ask?

I closed my eyes and sipped the lemon tea Phillip made. This was not the time to interrogate the person who was helping me.

"You are quiet," Philip said. The worst thing he could say

when I was trying to tamp down my suspicious brain. "You can ask me anything or tell me whatever is bothering you."

"I guess I'm thinking about all the work ahead of me," I said, which was the truth, too.

"We're all here to help," he said. "You'll need to make some decisions, but after that, people will make it happen."

"Is the building going to take weeks?" And then what? A business wasn't successful just because it existed. And how many decisions do I need to make?

"No. It all goes pretty smoothly here. If there are some unique fittings, you'll need to wait for them to come from the mainland. Is that all?"

Did he read my mind?

"Is the island accessible all year? I mean, there are plenty of storms in the winter. Time is slipping by and if I can't get guests until spring, I'll still need to work to pay the council."

"D tells us when there's a big one coming. But you'll have clients from Henbane to cover the times when mainlanders can't come."

His answer settled a worry, but that just meant the others expanded to fill the space. He was in such a talkative mood that I hoped I could ask about the mentor thing. Since I'd decided to put things magical on hold, maybe that was my opening. "I don't understand what the mentorship thing is, really," I said, keeping my eyes on my tea so I wouldn't stop if I saw his reaction. "I guess I should tell you that I've decided to make The Inner Spell my priority, so finding my third power is going to wait, and I'll learn the spells I need to get the business going, but nothing else until I've got time.

He didn't radiate any emotions about my decision. He often managed to conceal his reactions from me, so I wasn't surprised. I looked up and he was smiling. So it wasn't as bad as I feared.

"I'm here to help you, Cossi. I've been hands-off up to now because I didn't want to overwhelm you. If that's your decision, I'll respect it. When you want me to get more involved, tell me."

That seemed wrong. As the mentor, he knew everything, and I didn't have any experience. How was I supposed to know when to ask for his help? Or was he trying to figure it out, too? I might be the first person to need this kind of help.

I guess I'd mull that over before bringing up the subject again. "Okay, let's see if I can understand how you find books, and how to reach out to witches who live outside Henbane. We have that in common; most of my clients will be living among the non-magical people."

No one came into the shop for the rest of the afternoon. Not unusual, because Phillip did most of his business online. He showed me how to enter the magical part of the internet, kind of like the dark net, but for all kinds of magic users, and people. And, as far as I know, no hit men or drug deals.

I already had the access codes from D, but we hadn't managed a session that taught me the best way to use what was a shadow-world version of the normal internet. Social media of all kinds. Storefronts, even something like *Reddit* but with topics that ranged from finding spell ingredients to fixing a spell gone wrong.

"I can't wait to get some pictures of The Inner Spell to post," I said. "I can start piquing interest as soon as the building starts."

He glanced at the front of the store. It was a couple of hours until he usually closed, so I checked to see if anyone was coming in. Nope. It was still light outside and it would be, even though the days were getting shorter.

"You should go now and get some 'before' pictures," he said. "If you don't, you can't do one of those progress videos."

"But shouldn't I keep learning?" He was right about 'before' pictures. And I'd almost missed the opportunity, but I could do it in the morning.

"Go now," he said. "When you get back, we'll grab dinner and then you can do the ledgers. You learn quickly, so I'm sure you'll have everything in hand by the time the building starts."

Like a kid with a surprise half-day off school, I took our tea things upstairs, grabbed my jacket, bag, and camera before heading for Beulah.

In twenty minutes, I was standing at the cabin-tents thinking about framing the pictures for the best effect.

"I'm coming," Destroyer shouted in my head. Why was it he could yell, but I kept being scolded for being loud?

"Because I am Destroyer and you are just a witch," the crow said as he landed on the ground at my feet.

"Where have you been?" I asked. "I haven't seen you for a couple of days."

"Doing crow things. You haven't needed me. I don't care to sit around learning lessons."

Fair enough. I told him what I planned to do, and he hopped to an off-camera position. "I am not a marketing tool."

Not sure why a crow in the picture would enhance the sales value, but I didn't argue. I took a picture that included one of the tent-cabins — I really needed to figure out a better name for them — then unlocked the door of the center one and took a photo and a short video of the interior. Now that I was doing the work, I could see the potential of showing the progress to potential clients.

"What do you think we should call these structures?" I asked Destroyer.

"How should I know?"

I ignored his tone and did a synonym search. "Bothy? That sounds ancient enough."

"Like bothyroom?"

"Okay, too close to bathroom, so not bothy. Why are you here?"

"Something is happening at the shifter village. You should go."

4

Like everything on Henbane, the shifter village was only a short ride, and the sun was still hours from setting. I'd built up some fitness now that the only way to get around was bike or feet. The problem was the Alpha, Dolph. I didn't know his last name, or even if he had one. Was alpha like diva, only one name needed?

I pulled my thoughts off the side track as I passed Sheena's bar, The Howling Place, and slowed my bike. The last time I was here, Dolph was fairly clear about not making me welcome. Most of the shifters I met, sure it was only two so far, were friendly. If Dolph didn't like me, I wasn't sure how long that would last.

Lance and Dolph had a history, and that affected our last investigation. I might be the only witch on the island who didn't know the details. It wasn't my business unless Lance decided I needed to know, and I'm pretty sure Dolph wouldn't tell me.

"What's the thing?" I thought toward Destroyer, "and where is it? I don't hear anything."

"A body," he said. "Near the Alpha's house. Mark is there."

I'd hoped that this week would pass without a dead body. Maybe this one wasn't a murder. "Why did you send me here?"

"I thought you were bored." He swooped past me. "You are good at finding killers. We crows are curious and like to help."

I didn't believe help was what they liked. Mostly, Destroyer seemed to enjoy lording it over the other birds — and bossing them around.

"Do you know who?" I got off my bike and pushed it toward the fork in the road that held Dolph's house. As I got closer, I heard loud voices.

"No. In wolf, so we crows don't recognize them. If they talk to us, we know voices, but in wolf, they just look like dogs."

"Don't say that where you can be overheard," I said. I'd been here long enough to know shifters didn't like being called dogs.

"No human can hear me," he said. "Hurry."

I parked my bike next to a tree and walked toward the noise. Dolph's house was kind of in the middle of the village. Of course, I'd only been in as far as his place, so I might be wrong. Two shifters loped past me as I made my way but the house didn't come into sight until I was across the street from it. Some kind of cloaking spell that only affected non-shifters?

The yard was full. It was a large space, but a ring of shifters reached the fence. The fight was happening in the center, and it sounded like I'd arrived just as the shouting was turning into physical action.

I nudged my way through the shifters, hoping no one

would chase me away. When I got to the edge, I saw Mark and Dolph shouting at each other over the body. A white wolf, deep wounds tearing the fur on his, or her, flanks. Definitely dead.

"This is a murder," Mark said, his voice flat and calm. I guess he'd realized the yelling wasn't working.

"Aria is one of my pack," Dolph shouted. "My pack, my responsibility."

"Do you know how to investigate? Any suspects?" Mark kept his voice level and sounded a bit like he was willing to hand over the case if Dolph had a clue.

An older woman stepped from the crowd. She snarled at Dolph and then knelt beside the body. "She is my child," the woman said. "You are my Alpha, Dolph, but this man is the expert. Please let him find her killer. Her children need to know."

The pack muttered something, and I scanned the crowd for a way out. How stupid had I been, getting myself in the middle of a crowd of people who could tear me apart?

Dolph took in a deep breath, his eyes on the woman. I saw the fury just below the surface, but in my dealing with him, that was normal. To the others, he must seem calmer. He looked at Mark and then scanned the crowd. When he saw me, his lip curled in a sneer. So, not feeling the love. I reminded myself he wasn't just the shifter alpha; he was part of the governing council of Henbane.

"I will give you three days, because Leda asked," Dolph said. "You will keep me updated on the progress. You will use my people for tracking. If you have not solved this by then, I cannot promise anything."

Mark nodded. Was it important that he didn't speak?

Dolph told the crowd to disperse and then stalked back into his home.

Suddenly we were alone. The woman still sat beside her daughter's body, stroking the fur and sobbing. Mark watched her. I couldn't help from where I was standing, but there was no way I would let this murder go any more than the last two.

"Can I see?" I asked, hoping the woman wouldn't think I was just nosy.

Mark turned his gaze on me as if he hadn't known I was there. His emotions were overwhelmed by the mother's. Something new for my power. Up to now, I could read everyone individually.

"Stay there," he said, pointing to the ground where I was standing like he pinned me there with magic.

Just to be sure, I shuffled to the side. Nothing stopped me.

He bent down to talk to the mother. "Leda, I am so sorry this happened. I'll give you time with her, but I will need to examine everything. Let me know when you're ready."

She nodded but didn't take her eyes off the body.

He walked over to me and drew me farther away. "This is different," he said. "You heard Dolph. He's going to be all over the investigation."

"But you know I can help. I'm sure an animal somewhere saw or heard something."

"Shifter crimes are different," he said. "Mostly Dolph deals with them. He reports what happens to me, but I have no authority to stop him applying whatever justice he thinks is right in the small things."

"Is there a lot of shifter crime?"

"Petty stuff. That's why I got the three days. But if he decides I'm doing it wrong, or just gets impatient, he'll kick me off."

"I know the feeling," I said. Then regretting the words, I

added, "Look, you need all the help you can get. Do you think a shifter did this?"

"I don't know."

"Make him take your help," Destroyer said.

"I can't," I thought back. I guess Mark took my silence as acceptance because he told me to go home.

Well, he hadn't welcomed me into the last two murders either, so I'd go underground. Or maybe stay out of it. Yeah right.

5

I grabbed my bike and started home. Before I got ten feet, Lance stepped out of the trees. I pulled over. As a shifter, he might have a good idea of what's going on.

"Meet us at Sheena's," Lance said. "I don't want to talk out here where Mark will see us."

I agreed and rode the short trip to the bar. You'd think seeing a dead body, being surrounded by people who could turn into killer animals, and being told to mind your own business would kill your appetite. For me, it just made me hungry. Or the fact that using magic, or being in a magic place, burned calories.

Dinner at The Howling Place would go well with whatever gossip Lance and Sheena had for me. And for the first time, I wasn't worried about what I knew or didn't know about magical people. Did that mean I was getting used to murders, or just settling in here on Henbane?

I sent Phillip a text to say I was having dinner with friends, and I'd be home later to do the books. Then I remembered he'd said we'd eat together. Crap. Before I could send an apology, he responded with a happy face. I guess he didn't mind.

Sheena waved me to a table in the corner. "Lance is calling your friends, and he's already ordered."

He was an excellent predictor of what people needed when it came to food and drink. The first time Lance ordered for me and everyone at the table, I had to smother my annoyance. Such an alpha move. I could make my own food choices. Blah, blah. After that meal, I didn't complain.

I sat, and a waiter placed a cider and a glass of water in front of me. "Lance said the others will get here soon," he said. "Food when they arrive."

The drink was crisp and refreshing. I set it aside after a sip and drank water. I'd slake my thirst and save the alcohol for dinner. Probably not a good idea to turn up half cut for my session with the ledgers.

Lilibeth stepped through the open door and waved. D walked behind her to the table.

"Lance was mysterious," Lilibeth said. "Is this about the problem at the shifter village?"

"Do you know what it is?" D asked. "Mark hasn't reached out yet about setting up a case spreadsheet."

Should I take pleasure in being the first to have details? No, but I did. "Wait for Lance," I said.

"Who else is joining us?" D asked.

I hadn't noticed before that there were five chairs. "I don't know. Maybe this is just a bigger table than we need."

Lance handed ciders out and then nodded to Sheena. "Food when we've talked," he said. "It won't take long."

Sheena slid into the extra chair. She looked like an exotic painting. Hair long and wavy, green eyes that seemed to pull you in. Her skin was like porcelain, and she didn't wear makeup. All the shifters I'd met were like they'd been generated by AI with the prompt 'perfect looking' as the base.

"You were there," she said to me, "at the Alpha's."

"Destroyer told me to go," I said. "Did you know Aria?"

"She was a friend," Sheena said. "Shifters are hard to kill, Cossi. We don't have accidents, and we heal fast. I know you're new here, but this isn't just a murder. It's devastating. I'm asking you to investigate. All of you."

Wow. I must be getting a reputation as a detective. "Dolph gave Mark three days," I said. "He told me to stay out of it."

"Dolph will want it solved," Lance said. "He had no choice but to be aggressive with so many of the pack there. If he has to find the killer, he'll make a mess of it, and he'll have to answer to the council."

"Lance is right," Lilibeth said. "The alpha protects the pack. Dolph has his issues, but he can't turn away help. And he can't appear weak."

"We could try," D said. "This time we tell Mark everything we find."

I wanted to do as they asked. There was something behind all these killings, and I was fairly sure they had something to do with what my mother did. And Mrs. Vestum told me I was the trigger for the violence that started when I arrived. If she was right, I had an obligation to help stop it. Maybe only in my head, but I still wasn't willing to stay out.

"Let's say we try to keep him up to date," I said. "You know as soon as we hand over information, Mark will try to stop us."

Sheena pushed up from the table. "He won't have time to shut you down. With three days, he can't afford any distractions."

"And Dolph?" I asked. "I don't think he wants me involved. I'll take your word that he's all about protecting the pack, but he's still the alpha, and I can't just ignore him."

"I'll take care of him," Sheena said. "If you keep me updated, I can run interference with Dolph and the other pack members."

I'd been so worried about the alpha and the cop that I hadn't even considered that the other shifters might not want me on the case.

"Don't worry," Lance said. "We all want the killer found. And Dolph won't pull me off the case like last time. It'll look bad for him if he's not doing everything to get justice for Aria."

Sheena beckoned to someone near the kitchen and then went back to tending the bar. The waiter arrived with bowls of stew and a big platter of bread and vegetables. "Let me know if you need anything," he said, "and good luck."

How many of the shifters already knew we were on the hunt? And was the killer one of them? If shifters were hard to kill, it narrowed the suspects to some very dangerous types.

6

"This one is going to be harder," I said. "Phillip has me working like an intern in the bookstore. I'll have to find reasons to leave to investigate."

"The Inner Spell," D said. "You have to do site visits, right? We'll just use that as a base."

It sounded reasonable, but I'd learned that lots of pretty stupid things sounded reasonable before you got in too deep. We didn't have much choice, though, and I'd get a better idea of the work being done. "It's not a building site yet," I said. "But wandering around and thinking about what I want is a good excuse to be there. And I need a name for the tent cabin things. So you'll all have a reason to be there too."

"So, we start tomorrow?" Lance said. "No one will be officially investigating until then, anyway. We'll have Aria's memorial tonight, and she'll be burned as soon as Doctor Rene releases the body. We have different burial rites, but everything on this will be by the book."

For a place that never had murders, why would they create procedures? "Will she do an autopsy?"

"She'll take samples, just in case, but nothing intrusive. We stay in the form we die with," Lance said. "Any injuries that she got as a human before she died might not show in wolf form, but everything that happened in wolf form will show on her human body."

I tried not to think what parts of a human wouldn't be on the wolf. It was completely wrong to ask now, or maybe ever. And I had a feeling it wouldn't matter. Whatever killed her would show up.

"I guess if there's a memorial, you'll be able to attend, and then you can see if anyone is acting suspicious." I assumed only shifters would be welcome, so I had planned to spend the evening trying to come up with a starting point, after I did the bookstore ledgers and whatever else Phillip assigned to me. "Shall we meet early? Have breakfast at The Inner Spell?"

"I'll bring food," Lance said. "I'm not sure what I'll get from the memorial, but I will watch for clues. You think a shifter did this?"

"Let's not get stuck on a theory without any clues," I said.

"But who else could kill Aria?" Lilibeth asked. "She was strong and fast."

"The right spell could incapacitate her," D said. "We need to know if Doctor Rene finds anything like that, and what the actual cause of death is. I don't know how to get into her findings. And it's kind of a violation to hack into medical records anyway."

"I just sent a text offering my help," Lilibeth said. Her phone pinged and she glanced at it. "She's on her way there and doesn't want to do it alone. I'll bring the information tomorrow."

She finished her food and left us.

"I should go too," I said. "What do I owe for dinner?"

"Consider it payment for investigating," Sheena said. She'd approached the table without making any noise. "I'll be at the memorial. If I see anything, I'll let you know, Lance."

D followed me out after I thanked Sheena. We were headed in the same direction, and it was reassuring to have company since it was almost dark.

"I'm going to talk to Destroyer," I said. "We should stop somewhere before we hit the village."

"Call him to you," D said. "Talking to him while he's on your handlebars is safer than in your head."

Every time I thought I'd figured out how to communicate with my familiar, something came up to show me how wrong I was. "Destroyer, come and talk," I said aloud.

"I'm right here," he said in my mind and then cawed a warning as he dropped from the sky to my once again unprotected shoulder.

"We weren't moving. Why didn't you land on the ground?"

"Just keeping you alert. You need to set up some kind of perch on this thing. I can't grab onto anything but you."

I passed his answer on and D shrugged. "No idea how, but maybe your contractor can make something up?"

Beulah was going to look awful with something just stuck on her. "He's on my shoulder now. I'll give a perch some thought when we have time. Let's get going."

Riding with Destroyer on my shoulder was awkward, but better than nothing. I told him everything that happened. "Is there something your bird army can do to find us clues?"

"We can try," he said. "Was she killed in the Alpha's garden?"

I passed on the question to D, who had no answer.

"I didn't see a lot of the scene because of the crowds," I told Destroyer.

"We can swoop in and check," Destroyer said. "If that's not the place, we can look for blood and damage."

"I thought you couldn't find blood," I said.

He preened before answering, raising his wing and almost tipping me off the bike. "We birds are interested in this detective work. Not just crows. But you will still need to talk to the ground dwellers. Prey tends to run if we land to ask."

"Smart of them," I said. "No guarantee they'll survive after telling you what they know."

"Inconvenient, yes," Destroyer said. "I will start at dawn. Now, I must return and sleep."

I managed to stop the bike and put my feet on the ground for stability before he launched himself off my shoulder. I could see the pinpoints of blood staining my teeshirt. "I'm hoping my skin will toughen up enough soon."

"I don't think you can rely on him to keep to the same holes," D said. "Get some dressing on it when you get home."

"Are you going to search for clues?" I asked. "In the databases?"

"Without any direction, that won't help," he said. "I had an idea after the last case. We keep forgetting you don't know people here, so I thought I'd create a profile of Aria. Give you some history. Maybe doing that will shine a light on motives or something."

Phillip made no comment when I hurried into the kitchen hours later than we'd agreed. I didn't offer any excuse or apology. My desire to keep a secret overwhelmed my politeness.

"The ledgers are ready for you," he said, pointing to the

two hardbound books. "And your contractor dropped by earlier."

"He did? That makes it feel a lot more real. Is there a message?"

Inside the first book was a handful of receipts to be recorded. I had no idea why he kept a manual record because he also used the computer program. And I didn't see any discrepancies, not that I was all that skilled in financial crimes, to be sure.

"He'll meet you in the morning at the chalets to go over plans. I'll check your work tomorrow. You can focus your day on your own business."

So, he was a bit pissed at me. I didn't like disappointing him, but it did give us the day to work on the case. And he'd given the buildings their correct names — chalets, that's exactly what they were, even if the points were round.

7

M y contractor was Elias Jenkins. Despite the heat this early, he showed up in dungarees, plaid shirt and work boots. While you can never be sure of a witch's age, he appeared to be around fifty. Grey hair cut short, blue eyes and a stern expression. I felt all kinds of safe in his hands.

"You're new here, so I'll give you a fifty-cent lecture," he said. "I do the work, you make the decisions. I don't care for lots of changes, but I'll take care of what you need. I don't play games. When I tell you the deadlines, they are set in stone. The estimate will be approved by the council, and they'll have the final say on the costs for changes."

That might be a problem, but I wasn't going to try to anticipate it. *Live in the moment, Cossi.* "I guess there'll be delays for supplies," I said. "Everything comes from off-island, right?"

"Depends on what you want to do," he said. "I have what I need to repair the current structures. Maybe enough for some new construction, but don't worry. We have different supply lines than normals."

"So, is your crew available to work right away?" It would mean losing The Inner Spell for any secret meetings.

"Only two of us," he said. "We do it all. D will put in your computer stuff. We'll do plumbing and wiring."

He didn't leave much room for any more questions. "Where do we start?"

We spent an hour going over my expectations. The chalets needed plumbing and a few shelves. Mostly cleaning and stocking with linens and other necessities. The barracks were new, as well as a picnic area. While I talked, D and Lilibeth arrived and set up on one of the log circles.

Elias had been making notes the whole time, and when I said I'd run out of tasks, he made one final note.

"Sounds like a couple of weeks," he said. "You want it to look like this?" He drew a circle on the ground with his finger and a perfect image of The Inner Circle rose out of the dirt.

"Wow." It was all I could manage to get out. He'd captured my vision perfectly. I could see the little things that would become irritants over time. Like the barracks needed to be a bit farther from the chalets. "Yes, a few changes. When do I have to finalize it?"

"By the end of today if you want me to be available." He closed his hand and the vision disappeared.

After what seemed like forever trying to get approval — yes, I knew it was only a few weeks — everything felt rushed. I wouldn't have time to inspect my copy of the plans if we moved on the investigation. "What will happen if I want the barracks moved closer to the trees?" I asked. It was the only thing that jumped out at me.

"Plumbing cost increase, but not more than the council will okay. Why are you moving it?"

"This will be a place to meditate and experiment, and

probably research. I think leaving the barracks where it was closes the place in too much."

He grunted and did the spell again. This time the image showed the barracks almost tucked under the branches of the trees. Suddenly everything seemed more welcoming. "That's the place," I said. "Before you end the spell, is there any way I can get a photo?"

"Never done it before," he said. "Go ahead."

I pulled out my phone and took a shot of the model. Then I laid on the ground for another angle. When I stood and looked at the screen, the picture was clear, but the magic was gone. Just piles of dirt representing buildings.

Elias looked over my shoulder and muttered, "Needs color. Good idea though."

"At least I know what it should look like," I said. "The barracks should be in a lighter wood with darker accents. What else do you need from me to put the quote together?"

"I'll send you a list of questions about design," Elias said. "Tomorrow. Answer as quick as you can. Now go eat and leave me be."

He packed his things up and took a few soil samples before riding off. I joined D, Lilibeth, and Lance, who'd arrived with breakfast only a few minutes ago.

"Eat," Lance said. "The heating spell won't last long."

As soon as we were all holding coffee and breakfast sandwiches, I asked, "Any updates?"

Lilibeth took a sip of her coffee and then unwrapped her sandwich. "I didn't get to see Aria's body. Doctor Rene told me to work with Leda and help her control her grief. The woman just sobbed until the sedation spell took over. It's so awful. I know this isn't the first murder, but this one feels so much worse."

"Because it's a shifter?" Lance asked.

"Maybe." Lilibeth bit into her sandwich to avoid adding anything. I got the sense from her emotions that her answer was only part of the truth.

"So, we don't have a cause of death," I asked. "Any idea if she had enemies? That's the kind of question cops ask on TV."

"I offered to help with Mark's investigation, do some tracking," Lance said. "Dolph told me to leave it alone. Not like last time. It kind of seemed like he was telling me to work with you all behind Mark's back."

That wasn't great news. If everyone on the island thought we were better at solving crimes than the witch whose job it was, then Mark would shut us down.

"Are you sure?" Lilibeth asked. "That doesn't sound like Dolph."

"No, it doesn't." Lance bundled the wrapper and cup into the same bag they came in. "And I'll keep an eye on him."

"As a suspect?" I asked.

"No. He wouldn't kill one of his own," Lance said. "I meant as a pain in the butt. If he thinks we can be ordered around, he will push us in all kinds of directions."

"What do we do now?" D asked. "I didn't find anything in her background that would lead to murder, or enemies."

I could only think of one action. "How do we get a good look at where they found her body?"

8

_____

Sneaking around the Alpha's house wasn't an easy task. Dolph wasn't outside guarding the empty spot where Aria's body was found, but Mark was still there, and Doctor Rene, and a handful of shifters. We stood far enough away that no one would tell us to leave, and close enough to catch a few words.

"I can go in," Lance said. "It's possible I can convince the others you came to pay your respects."

"And Mark?" I asked. "I don't know if he'll let us get close."

"He won't," Lilibeth said. "We should come back later when he's gone."

I didn't want to leave. If I headed back to the bookstore, Phillip would find me something to do. With only three days to solve it, we couldn't risk losing any time.

"Lance, you go in. And, D, you can pretend to have questions about security and ideas to upgrade it. I have an idea that will only work if Mark doesn't see me."

We watched the two of them head towards the garden,

and then I drew Lilibeth far enough away that we wouldn't be seen.

"What's your plan?" she asked. "There's no spell to make us invisible, if that's what you're thinking."

Disappointing. I guess reading books about boy wizards wasn't a good grounding for real magic. "At least that means no one can spy on us. No creepy stalkers we can't see," I said. "I was thinking about using my language power and asking some animals to look for clues."

"What clues?" Lilibeth asked. "And what animals? You said they mostly can't figure things out like we do. They need specific questions."

I hadn't thought it through that well. And I didn't want to admit it to her because I knew it was exactly what she thought about me. It wasn't great to be able to read the emotions of my friends. Maybe when I had a better handle on magic and my powers, I'd know how to tell them to keep everything hidden from me. That magical day when I'd understand all my magic was getting pushed further and further into the future. Good thing witches lived for centuries.

"I was thinking Destroyer," I said, "and a few of his friends. He might be able to overhear something, and he could get a peek in through the windows to see what Dolph is up to."

"That's a great idea. I wish I had a familiar who could help us solve cases."

She was great with animals, but none had asked to be her familiar — yet.

"I'm actually wishing we don't get any more cases," I said.

"We can't control that," Lilibeth said. "Get Destroyer on the job."

I felt weird talking to Destroyer in my head while Lilibeth was standing next to me, but the risk of being overheard was too high to do it aloud.

"What do you think we'll see?" he asked when I called.

"Maybe see if there is anything unexpected on the ground," I said. "At least how much blood was left behind. That way we'll know if she was killed there."

"Roy's witch doesn't think so," Destroyer said. "Don't you think all the clues will be gone?"

"Probably, but it's better for us to know," I said. "Did Roy tell you anything else?"

"He didn't tell me anything."

Even in the short time we'd been familiar and witch, Destroyer had found a way to irritate me. I knew he was doing it on purpose, because sometimes he answered my questions with all the details, and others he made me dig for every iota.

"Who told you Aria wasn't killed in Dolph's garden?"

He swooped in and landed on the ground at our feet. "If you are interested in the tiniest of details, no one told me. I was near when he said it to the Alpha. He said the doctor expected more blood on the ground, so they were right about it being a message to the Alpha."

"You can understand other witches?" Had I completely missed something? Probably, but now wasn't the time to think back on all our conversations.

"Since I talk to you, I recognize the words when others talk. Only the kind you speak."

That made him a way more valuable sneak. "Just you?" He'd been training other animals to search for people and bring us evidence from crime scenes.

"Only the crows," he said. "We are the only animals

intelligent enough to learn such things. Now, what do you think I will find?"

I updated Lilibeth on the conversation, hoping she'd come up with a way to tell Destroyer how to identify a clue.

"It's a kind of 'know it when you see it' thing, right?" Lilibeth glanced past my shoulder. "The boys are back."

Lance and D joined us, both saying hi to Destroyer as soon as they noticed him.

"We got told to leave," Lance said. "I couldn't scent anything while we were there."

"Dolph came out as soon as we arrived," D said, "didn't even give me a chance to talk to Mark."

"I'll send Destroyer in to eavesdrop," I said. I looked for him on the ground, but he'd gone. I hadn't seen him fly off. I'd get a lecture from him later on the proper way for a witch to be aware of her familiar. "Where did you go?" I thought the words at him.

"Not now. Wait there," he said back.

"Apparently he's too busy to help," I said. "I guess we need to find another way to get ahead."

"Impatient witch," Destroyer said. "I am listening. This is what the doctor said. 'Cause of death was the blow to her head, but all the injuries before that weakened her.' I have been shooed away from the garden. Impertinent shifters."

"We need to get at the doctor's autopsy reports," I said.

9

"How?" Lilibeth asked. "You can't send raccoons to steal it, right? Animals can't read, so they can't tell you."

Details. It was always the details that got in the way. "I was actually thinking we might sneak in and have a look. Take pictures if we're in a rush."

"So we're going from amateur investigators to cat burglars?" Lance said. "We'll get caught. And then Mark will have to put us in a cell to keep us from getting in his way."

"How protected will it be?" I asked. "In my old world, they were online but under hard-to-break security. At least, that's what I think. I was hoping there would be a magic way to get a peek."

"We can't stay here if we're going to plan a break-in," Lilibeth said. "Let's get back to my place."

"So you think we can do it?" I asked.

"No. I think you're crazy. But we can think more clearly over a coffee, and no one will be eavesdropping." She retrieved her bike and told us to hurry up.

While we rode, I had plenty of time to think through

how I'd made the leap to searching a doctor's records. It wasn't frustration. Or, not only that. It was the deadline. Dolph said three days, and we were almost halfway through day one with nothing but one clue. She was killed somewhere else. Not the first time we had to find a kill site. And Destroyer would get someone on finding that faster than I could find a carrion eater who'd cooperate.

I might not be the cause of all the killing, but Mrs. Vestum was right; my arrival flicked a switch or pulled a trigger. So far, two witches were dead, and now a shifter. Regardless of what happened with Aria's case, I was going to get to the bottom of that.

We got to Run, Fly, Slither before I could figure out my first step in researching the secrets behind the killing. I did know I needed to talk to Mrs. Vestum, and the idea of going to her for help made me a little ill. Who wants to work with someone who hates them?

Lance bought us coffee from Jan's place, and we sat in Lilibeth's small office, ready for the ideas to flow. Unfortunately, the muse didn't cooperate.

"What about Roy?" Lance said. "Will he tell you anything?"

"The bond is too strong," Lilibeth said. "He can't go against Mark's instructions."

"And he told me before he wouldn't," I said.

"You can still ask," D said. "If Mark didn't expressly say to keep you in the dark, there's a loophole."

"Like when Lance helped us find Jeffery?" I asked. "I'll reach out, but don't hold your breath."

"So, what do we know about Aria?" Lilibeth asked. "Knowing the victim; isn't that the first thing cops do?"

Every time they asked me about what cops did, I felt like they expected me to know everything about mundane human life. I'd never even dated a cop. Well, until Mark. I guess what we were doing was dating.

"Your information comes from the same place mine does," I said. "Books and cop shows. But it's common, so maybe it's a good place to start. It's not like we have anything else."

"I checked my databases and our social media last night," D said. "I created a profile but it's not all that deep because it's all from online sources."

"It's way better than nothing," I said, "and we have to start somewhere."

"She worked with the pups to train them to run with the pack instead of just tearing around. She sold tip sheets to shifters in other communities. She didn't have any confrontations online or any complaints about or from anyone."

"Aria was a nice person," Lance said. "In or out of wolf, she was always there to help anyone who needed guidance. She counseled Dolph."

"What does that mean?" I asked.

"You think the Alpha is some kind of dictator," Lance said. "No. He has the last word, and the pack obeys his wishes. But four or five of us advise him. He's our moral compass, so no one wants to let an alpha get too controlling."

The whole alpha thing was a complete mystery to me. Lance and Dolph were apparently rivals for the position, and Lance stepped back, so Dolph took the job. Lilibeth knew what happened, and I'm guessing any witches who were interested at the time also knew. No one talked about it, and I didn't have the guts to ask for the story.

"Her own children are grown, and her mother is the

only parent left," D said. "Her father died almost twenty years ago. Accident in the forest."

There was that timeline again — almost twenty years ago, my mother made a mistake that forced them to leave the island. "Was Aria a friend of my parents?"

"I couldn't find any indication," D said. "She knew Mrs. Macy from the store. Aria foraged for some of the more difficult-to-find ingredients. She also knew Zeke, but it's a small island, Cossi; we all know each other to some degree."

"Not enough to know why people are committing murder," Lilibeth said. "Maybe we should start by talking to Aria's mother. Or do you think Dolph would run us off, Lance?"

"He won't be happy, but Leda might not want to talk," Lance said. "And I don't think we should intrude on her grief."

I agreed with him. Mark was the only one with an excuse to talk to her, and it was cruel to ask her questions. "I'll see what I can get out of Roy," I said. "If we don't know what happened to her before she died, I'm not sure we can even help Mark, let alone solve the crime."

10

_____

I needed to put in some time in at the bookstore, but I still had an hour or so before Phillip would expect me. He might know that Elias was long done with me, but I could be thinking about my business, right?

Destroyer told me Roy was with Mark, so I couldn't even try to get information from him. And I'd put money on the fact we'd know exactly what happened to Aria when we found the spot where she'd been murdered. Shifters were strong, fast, and healed almost instantaneously. However the killer did it, they would have weakened her with a potion or a spell, first. Or there were multiple killers. Or... I didn't know enough about Henbane's inhabitants to keep guessing. It felt a little gratifying when no one else could come up with anything either.

I got out Beulah and headed back to the shifter village. I might not be able to talk to Leda or Dolph. The Alpha's garden was also off limits, but I had an edge. If I could talk to any of the animals around the house, I might learn how Aria's body was placed in Dolph's yard. 'Why' would be better, but 'how' would give us a starting point.

I came alone because I didn't want to explain or answer questions, and one person was easier to hide than two. I hoped the shifters were too busy to sniff me out. They could easily, but I'd learned that, like me with reading emotions, they chose to ignore scents unless they needed to find someone.

Maybe this time, a shifter would find the murder site. Unless there was spell on it like the last case, or it was really isolated like Mrs. Macy's murder.

I parked Beulah at The Howling Place, pretty sure that Sheena wouldn't mind. The walk to Dolph's was only around ten minutes, and I didn't need to get right next to it. One benefit of sneaking around Henbane was that other than the main village street, trees grew everywhere. I sat at the base of a chestnut and stilled my mind.

"Are there any animals near me who know about the dead shifter?" The words were all in my mind. No one was likely to pay attention to any creature who responded, but my talking aloud would give the game away.

"Why?"

I looked around and saw a squirrel on the trunk just above me. One day, I would think a bit more about what kind of animal I wanted. Up to now, squirrels had been my main source of information, but they always wanted to bargain.

"Did you see what happened?" I thought at her or him. I couldn't really tell the sexes apart by sight.

"What's it worth to you? You're that witch with the food, right?"

"Food for information, yes." This was the first time I'd gotten attitude. I guess living around people who could shift into wolves made you a bit more aggressive.

"I didn't see myself. I know someone who did. You pay me for bringing her, and you pay us?"

"What's your name?"

"You won't be able to say it. Call me Joe. Answer the question."

Had I created this level of intermediary? I hoped not, but since I was the only one who could talk to animals, at least right now, maybe I was the culprit.

"Yes. I have enough food to pay you both."

"Wait."

I did as I was ordered. If this didn't pan out, I'd call someone else. Or if the squirrel forgot, not likely with a promise of food, I could try again. I'd wondered if I was creating a dependency but was laughed at when I asked.

The sounds of life in the shifter village drifted in an out as I sat there enjoying a moment of peace. This is the kind of vibe I wanted at The Inner Spell. Not silence, but quiet.

A few snippets of conversation caught my attention.

"Leda is resting..."

"Can't find it again..."

"Not one of us..."

"...strong enough to..."

"... things are getting out of control..."

Nothing I could use, but also, reassuringly, nothing reaching the level of anger. I guess hoping I'd hear someone confess was stupid.

The shifters seemed to accept this was Mark's job. I wished I could do that, but my mother was part of this, and I couldn't just sit and wait for whatever that meant for me.

"This is my mate," Joe said. "Call her Al."

So, his choice of name had nothing to do with gender. It didn't matter because I wasn't going to be that involved in their lives. I pulled a handful of seeds and nuts from my backpack. "Tell me what you know, and this is yours."

"Where is my payment?" Joe asked, skittering to stop Al approaching.

"This is how it will work," I said. "Al tells me what she knows, and I pay her. Then I pay you. If the information is helpful, I'll add more."

I would have to spend some time coming up with a payment system, at least for these creatures. Other animals hadn't been so interested in negotiating. I had no idea if that would change.

"No. This is how it will work," Joe said. "You pay me now. Al tells you her information and then you pay her. I get more if the information is helpful."

I didn't want to sit here bargaining for hours. "I'll give you half. She tells me the information. I pay her, if the information sounds helpful, I pay you the rest. No bonus."

"Stop it," Al chittered at both of us. "She is generous. We won't need to find food today, and we want the shifter's death avenged."

"You knew her?" I didn't realize the shifters made friends with the forest animals.

"If someone could do that to a shifter, what chance do we have?" Al said.

So I'd gotten it wrong again.

"Okay, what's the scoop?" I regretted it as soon as I said it. How stupid did I sound?

"We saw them put her body in the big shifter's garden," Al said.

11

———

"Who did it? When?" The words bubbled out of my mouth.

"More food," Joe said.

"Last night, not late," Al said. "We were going to the secret place where we store food. Two shifters. Big. Male. They were in human form. We don't know them much."

It was beyond them to identify individuals, but there must be some detail to help me. "That's good information," I said. "Did you see anything that could help me find them?"

"More food," Joe said with a glare at Al.

"More food," Al said. "This is new deal."

I offered a second handful, not caring about the cost.

"Looked same," Al said. "Not same same, but could be from same grandparents. Tall, one yellow hair, one red."

"Did they say anything?"

"Said she shouldn't be left to be eaten by animals," Joe said. "That's all. Now pay me, too."

"Are you going to eat it all now?" I asked as I put a pile of seeds and nuts on the ground.

"Joe guard. I hide," Al said.

"If I put it in a bag, could you carry it?" If the price of information was going up, it probably made sense for me to carry packages.

"Small bag." Al stared at me as if expecting me to produce one.

"I'll bring one next time," I said. "One more question?"

"We don't know more," Joe said.

"Not about the shifter," I said. "How did you understand the shifters when they spoke?"

"Predators." Al gathered up handfuls of the food and scurried away.

"You go," Joe said. "Too loud. Others will come."

I pushed myself up and thanked him. Time to head off to make what I could of the information.

The challenge I faced now was just that. I didn't know enough shifters to identify a red-haired and blond cousin set. And I didn't want to ask Lance directly because for one thing, he was a redhead, and the other was I couldn't quite convince myself he wouldn't run off and confront them. He had disobeyed Dolph and kept with us on the last case.

All I had was the short conversation Al overheard. The two might not be killers or accomplices. They moved the body, yes, but because they wanted her found. And they knew where she was killed — unless the murderer dumped her on the side of the road. And as far as I was aware, they hadn't told Mark or Dolph.

I headed over to The Howling Place to talk to Sheena. She didn't fit the description, being female and raven-haired, and she might just have a tip to deal with Lance.

I sat at the bar because it was where Sheena worked, and because the tables were all full. When I walked in, most people stared, but the conversations continued. I tried to ignore the feelings that washed over me. Fear, hurt, curiosity, a full gamut from everyone. Not one ounce of guilt, which was interesting but not helpful. If the killer thought the murder was justified, then it wouldn't occur to them to feel guilt.

"Let's go into my office. I've got a privacy spell bag in there," Sheena said when I asked her for some advice. "Too many perked ears here today."

I picked up my cider and followed her into a small room off the kitchen. It held a desk and three chairs. A couple of filing cabinets stood in the back corners. A laptop rested on one, a clock and coffee maker on the other.

Sheena sat in one of the visitor chairs and pointed to the other. It was a more intimate choice than having the desk between us.

I put my glass on a coaster and took a breath. Lance's power was working with wood, and he'd had a big hand in designing the space. I caught the aromas from the kitchen mixed with beeswax and cedar.

"What do you need from me that you can't get from Lance?" Sheena asked. "It's not a problem, Cossi. He can be a bit hot-headed, but he's not going to do anything rash."

"I found out something today and I'm worried about how he'll react. I'm also not sure if Mark and Dolph have heard."

"And you don't want to tell them if it means you'll get ahead in the case." Sheena laughed. "Hey, competition is a good thing. Tell me what you know. I promise not to go behind your back to anyone. If I think they should know against your wishes, I'll tell you what I plan to do."

Oddly comforting words. "Your power is to see things that are going to happen, right?"

"It's not reliable unless I focus. I would not have been able to see that Aria was in danger, but if you ask a specific question, I might be able to help."

"Won't me knowing change the prediction?" It couldn't be that easy, even on a magical island.

"There are two kinds of... categories is the best word, but it's not completely right. Some things can't be stopped. Some things can — under the right conditions."

I told her the news and asked if she knew whether Mark or Dolph were aware of any of it.

"As far as I know, they don't," she said. "They should."

"I'll let them know," I said. "Do you have any idea who they might be?"

"You saw the crowd outside," she said. "Too many shifters fit the 'cousins who look alike and are red-haired and blond'. It's a bit of a closed gene pool, overall. We bring in new blood every generation, but shifters kind of run to really hot looking."

That didn't help. "I guess someone will know if there's a more likely pair, right?"

"Your best bet is to tell Mark, who'll talk to Dolph. D might have some way to search for likelihood, but I can't give you any names without a lot more information."

"What happens if I keep the information to myself, or I guess just me, D, Lilibeth, and Lance?"

"And me," she said. "You can't untell me."

I nodded and waited for her to do some kind of trance or something.

She looked at the ceiling for a couple of minutes, then turned to me. "You look like you're expecting me to say something like 'the future is cloudy, and I need more money to clear the view'."

I spat the mouthful of cider I'd taken back into the glass and gasped a laugh.

"All I see is trouble if you keep the secret. Maybe trouble solving the case, or more likely, trouble with Dolph."

12

I headed home with Sheena's words echoing in my brain. What kind of trouble did she mean?

How much did I know Lance, really? Is there a remote chance he was the red-haired shifter? I had to believe he was innocent. And Dolph? No, the pack wouldn't let him get away with it.

"Destroyer," I called as I pulled off the path so I wouldn't get in the way of anyone coming past, even though there was no traffic. Riding and talking to him was too much for me this evening. Maybe I'd get used to it someday.

"I'm sorting out our searchers," he said. "What do you want?"

"Advice," I said. "Do you give it? Or is our relationship about doing each other favors?"

"What advice?"

I told him what Sheena said. "Do you think Lance could be involved?"

"You know him better than me," Destroyer said. "What if he is?"

Good question. If he wasn't, then telling Mark wouldn't

make much difference. If he was, then Mark was the best person to handle it.

"I'm worried about the Alpha," I said. "He and Lance already have a bad relationship. If Dolph learns Lance might be involved, then he might not look for the real culprit."

"Why aren't you asking the other witches? I thought they were your friends."

Apparently, Destroyer didn't consider himself a friend. And I was being a bad one to Lance. Of course he didn't kill or move Aria. Okay. I need to tell my friends, and we decide what to do. Sheena didn't say I had to tell Dolph and Mark, just that keeping it a secret would be trouble.

"I get the point," I said. "I'll talk to you later."

I HEADED HOME and Phillip set me up with the online order system. "I don't know how much you'll need to know about fulfilling orders," he said, "but there are ten in the queue. When you've done that, you can go back to whatever you were doing."

It wasn't hard work. Make note of all the books ordered. Find them on the shelves or do some research to find them elsewhere. Reply to the customers. Pack the books for mailing and check the box that the order was filled. It wasn't exactly mentoring, but I guess it was something.

I sent a text to Lilibeth, Lance, and D to meet me at Jan's. I was going to come clean. The weight of this one secret outweighed any time I'd kept one from my friends in the past.

"IT WASN'T ME," Lance said as soon as I passed on Al's news.

"We know," Lilibeth said. "There's too many who match."

"That's what Sheena said." I told them about her prediction.

Of course, now that I'd spilled my secret, I had nothing to offer. This might be one we wouldn't solve.

"Call Mark," Lilibeth said. "Roy will come with him. You might get an idea of that autopsy."

He told us to wait. No indication of how long.

"Do you have an alibi?" I asked Lance. "No one thinks you had anything to do with moving her body. But you might have to prove it."

"I don't," he said. "Thanks for thinking no one suspects me. I bet Dolph hopes he can use this to keep me under control."

Lance was the most controlled person I'd met in either of my lives. As a mundane, I'd met a lot of people who had a hard time keeping in their anger, but now that I thought of it, it's possible that it was my power telling me things others didn't know. The few glances I had of Lance's emotions told me he was like the Hulk; always angry.

"He wouldn't do that," Lilibeth said. "If you tell us what you were doing that night, we can figure out a way to prove your innocence."

"I was sleeping," he said. "Alone."

On the mainland, that might put him on the top of the suspect list, but now I could talk to all kinds of creatures; I knew we were never alone. Even with the spell bag keeping people out, I often found a spider or a fly in my room.

"I guess you don't have a pet," I said. "I can come around to your place and see who was flying or skittering around while you slept."

"We just need to find a way to convince Mark so he can

get Dolph to believe you are innocent." D opened his phone and made a note. "I've added it to our activities list. I saw on a show that the cops would create action lists every morning based on the knowledge they had of the crime."

This case was getting way more complicated than the others. Not only did we need to find the killer, we had the two shifters who moved the body, clearing Lance's name, and keeping Dolph off our backs. And now we had two days before something happened.

"What will Dolph do if Mark hasn't found the culprit in two days?"

Lilibeth shrugged. "Who knows? Maybe he'll have calmed down by then. He was furious when we saw him. It was like he thought someone was threatening him by putting her body there."

"We know that's not true," D said. "Cossi's informant said they wanted her to be found."

I had informants. I wasn't sure I liked the idea. My life here was about The Inner Spell and learning about my witch powers. Not forming a police department.

"What informant?" Mark asked as he pulled up a chair.

13

How I wish my power was knowing when someone was creeping up on me. And why did I sit with my back to the door?

"Do you want something to eat?" I asked, hoping for time to get my story together in my mind.

"I'm busy trying to find Aria's murderer before Dolph starts interrogating everyone on the island," he said. I guess that was the answer to my question. "What informant, Cossi? Please don't hold anything back."

"We're trying to help," Lilibeth said in our defense.

The emotions racing at my power were too much for me to sort out. Guilt, not for the murder but something about feeling useless. That could be any of us. Fear, I guess I understood that one. Only a fool wouldn't be a little afraid of killers roaming free. Impatience, weariness, lots of frustration. I guess the emotions were easy to sort out, just not who was feeling them.

"I know you're trying to help," Mark said. "I guess I need it, but don't get in the way, okay?"

It wasn't an invitation to join him, but at least he didn't tell us to stand down or he'd lock us up.

"Where's Roy?" I asked. I couldn't talk to him long distance like with Destroyer.

"Following a trail we found." He rubbed his face, and I felt the exhaustion flow from him. "Can you just tell me what you found?"

I told him about what Al and Joe saw. "They can't tell one shifter from another," I said. "But they can understand them."

"And you think it's Lance?" he asked, making the leap without any hint from us.

"It's not," I said. "Sheena told me there are too many shifters who fit the description."

"I was sleeping," Lance said. "That's my statement, so I'm sorry I can't help."

"I'll go look for an animal to ask," I said. "Someone to corroborate his alibi? Is that right?"

"Good thing I can tell when you're lying to me," Mark said. "Any chance some mouse will lie to you?"

"No animal has so far," I said. "I guess it's possible, but why would they?"

"To get food," Lilibeth said. "Sorry, I guess I shouldn't have said that."

"What else can we do to help out?" I asked before Lilibeth could say anything more.

"Is your familiar going to be helpful?" he asked. "Unless Roy finds anything, we're going to rely on shifters to search. If they were involved even in moving her body, I can't use them. And until I have to, I am not telling Dolph. He'll just go off on a rant and half the shifters will be locked up for no reason."

"What about his deadline?" Lance asked.

"As long as I'm finding some clues, he'll stay out of the way. So, I've got longer, but this needs to be solved fast."

"I'll ask Destroyer what they can do," I said, not mentioning the fact he was already on the case. "It would help if we knew the cause of death. Like how much blood we might find. If there's likely to be a lot of damage at the site."

Mark looked at each of us in turn. He'd locked down his emotions again, but he was definitely trying to figure out if we could be trusted. After a moment, he relaxed the tension he'd been holding in his entire body.

"There will be a lot of damage," he said. "There was definitely a fight, but whoever killed her managed to get poison into her blood or a spell on her spirit. Whatever happened, something weakened her enough to allow them to end her life."

"Thanks," I said. "It helps to know it wasn't a spell. Does Doctor Rene know what poison? Would it have an odor? Something an animal might need warning about?"

"We don't know yet," he said. "Be careful, it could be something from the mundane world. I don't want more bodies showing up."

He left us to mull over the information and make our plans. The first thing I needed to get my head around was the fact he'd just told us critical information, and Lance was a viable suspect until I got proof he was home.

"He must be really discouraged to tell us that," D said. "What do we do with it?"

"I'll update Destroyer," I said. "And he can find out if there's an animal who hangs around your place when you sleep, Lance. That will save us some time."

"If all we can do is wait for a lead," Lance said, "I guess we can go back to our day jobs and stay ready for action."

"You know, I never thought running my business was anything but my job," Lilibeth said. "Now I have a day job and a side gig?"

"Let's hope this is the last time we need to help Mark find a killer," D said. "I'm going to try some research on shifters who meet the description. Cousins who might be willing to move a body."

"I wonder why they didn't tell Mark about Aria? Why they needed to move her to Dolph's property was a mystery, too." Was there some shifter custom I didn't know about?

"That's a very good question," Lance said. "It would be normal to do what you said. If someone made them move the body, we have another lead to follow. I just don't know how we find proof without finding the shifters."

"And I guess Dolph won't just sit back and let us poke around the village," I said. "Are you all cousins?"

Lance looked at me like I was nuts.

"No, that wouldn't be good for the pack."

"But lots of cousins, right? How many kids in a family?"

I stuffed down the feeling I was being rude. Murder investigations meant questions people didn't want to answer.

"One or two," Lilibeth said. "Like humans, Cossi."

I figured it wasn't exactly that way, but decided it wasn't my business unless a shifter told me.

14

W hen I got home and settled in my room where, thanks to the spell bag, no one could come in and interrupt, I made a quick list of what I needed to accomplish. I didn't want to get distracted, and every task was important, so I couldn't risk forgetting something.

Find a way to prove Lance didn't move the body, find the murder site, find who moved Aria and why.

"Destroyer," I called in my mind.

"What? It's sleeping time," he croaked. "We start searching tomorrow."

"Good, but I have news." I brought him up to date. "Is there a way to find me a source to prove Lance was sleeping?"

"Go there now and see who's about," he said. "I don't have time to talk to mice. And they run from birds, anyway. Too stupid to realize we don't all like a furry snack."

I suppose I could head over to Lance's house. He lived near The Howling Place. I'd only been there once, but I could find it. "And searching for the murder site," I asked, "do you think the new information will help?"

I swear he pretended to yawn. Did crows yawn? I couldn't picture it.

"Yes," he said, after making me wait. "More can look. Not just blood, but damage. Maybe someone heard it happen."

"That would be a great help if they can tell me," I said.

"Most likely they ran from the noise. But we can see. You talk to ground animals, we deal with who flies. We will solve this case."

I let him get to sleep. Our deadline was fast approaching, and I felt every second tick past despite Mark's assurance that progress would keep Dolph in line. The birds would be searching before the sun rose, and I wasn't restricted to daylight. I sent a text to Lance asking if I could come over.

He answered right away. *Working right now. People are sharing theories in the bar. My place isn't locked. Come by when you're done.*

The apartment was quiet when I slipped out. Phillip was out or already asleep. I checked that my phone was charged because I needed the light to see my way, and I didn't know where Phillip kept flashlights if he even owned one. I had about a fifty percent charge, so I would be fine.

The bike parking lot was lit by what I assumed were spells. One came on as I stepped through the entrance, and others lit my way as I headed toward Beulah.

Riding with one hand holding my phone was hard. I probably should have walked but I wanted to get to his house as quickly as I could. I added a headlight to my list of things to order or buy the next time I was on the mainland.

I managed to get to Lance's without falling off or riding over the edge of the path. His place was what I'd call a tiny house. More like a camper than a cabin, everything inside had its place. Kitchen, living room, and bathroom on the main floor. His bedroom was on a mezzanine reached by a series of steps that disguised drawers in the risers.

I sat on the love seat after I closed the door. I turned the light on my phone down a little because I figured nocturnal creatures didn't enjoy bright lights. When my eyes adjusted to the dimness, I said, "Is anyone here who could say if the shifter was here two nights ago?"

I caught a scrabbling in the first step to the bedroom. "There's no danger, and I have food to pay."

"What food?" The voice came from beside me on the couch. A white mouse crouched low to the cushion as if ready to run at a second's notice.

"Seeds and nuts." It seemed to be a common food for all my sources.

"You mean the shifter who lives here with us?"

Lance would probably want to change that description.

"Yes. Can you tell shifters apart?"

"This one is our pet. Others are just different from him."

Good enough for the alibi. "Do you know about the shifter who was murdered?"

"Bad thing. Yes. Now many shifters are searching and we must hide more."

"Was your pet sleeping here all night?"

"Snoring, too. He snores loud. That night we heard shifters walking past. I looked because I am brave. They were carrying a heavy thing. Did not wake our shifter. Maybe magic because he is usually very alert."

"What is your name?" I figured it would sound more legitimate if I had a name to apply to my source.

"Means 'pretty' in your words," he said. "Food now?"

"Okay, I'll call you Pretty. Where can I put the seeds and nuts?"

He ran to a spot beside the first step. I saw a tiny hole was chewed in the side. I placed the handful of food near the hole and thanked him.

I didn't wait around because Lance needed to know he was in the clear. And I had more than I expected. If the two who moved Aria's body used magic, that might be traceable. And I had their path.

15

I needed sleep so I could juggle all my tasks. I expected the quote to come through any minute from Elias, and Phillip would be showing me some other business process in the morning. And even though we'd made progress on the case, we still didn't have anything to show us who the killer or killers were. That didn't even take into account all the magic I needed to learn about.

I couldn't work on much before I went home to bed, but Lance needed to know my news. I cycled the few meters to The Howling Place and found Lance tending bar.

"I can't stay," I said, "but you have your proof." I told him about the mice and promised to swear on whatever Dolph needed to make him understand it was true.

"He doesn't know I'm on Mark's suspect list yet," Lance said. "I have no idea how up to date he is with the case, either."

Surely Mark reported every step forward to keep Dolph from interfering. "There isn't a lot, but if he doesn't know you were a suspect, he won't know about the two shifters moving Aria. Can you find a way to tell him you are in the clear without getting Mark into trouble?"

Lance filled a beer order for the waitress before coming back to me.

"You want something to drink?" he asked.

I don't know why he was pretending he wasn't worried. He knew I could read him. And he could have shielded against my power, but he let me see everything. "I can't. It's dark and I have to ride one-handed, so I need my brain fully functioning."

He filled a beer glass with water. "This might help."

"What's the problem?" I really didn't want to wait for him to work it through. Everything seemed to be under a tight deadline tonight. My rational side knew it wasn't, unfortunately the emotional side was in control. "We can figure it out if you tell me."

He glanced down at the bar top for a moment. "I can't talk here." He called the waitress over and told her he was taking a break. "Ten minutes. I promise."

I took my glass of water and followed him around the side of the bar. A picnic table was set up under the cover of the eaves. He sat and patted the bench next to him. "Okay, we should be safe from nosy shifters here."

"So spill." I gulped down half the water to stop me from taking over the conversation. Lance was the one with the problem. I needed to listen first.

"A few things," he said. "The easiest is the mice. Do I owe them anything? I mean, they saved my reputation. I owe them for that, but I have no idea what they think I owe."

That one was easy. "Let them live with you. Feed them occasionally. I paid them, so I think they aren't expecting anything else."

He shuddered. "I was hoping I could build them a home

in my yard. But I guess I've been living with them for a while, so I can just keep going."

I could understand his reaction. I wouldn't want to know I was living with animals that could chew through wires either. And I guess mice carried diseases. "I can ask them, if you like."

"Let's wait until this is over," he said. "Dolph is the other problem. Maybe Mark is keeping things from him on purpose. I can't. He's my alpha and I have to tell him, Cossi."

I agreed with him. "I have no idea why Mark isn't updating him. It seems like telling him everything will stop Dolph taking over. I haven't passed on the information yet. I thought I'd do it tomorrow morning when I can have a conversation."

"I could hold off until morning," Lance said. "Dolph won't be happy, but it's good news so maybe he won't punish me."

"No. You should tell him." I pulled out my phone. "I'll call Mark now. If you can give him enough time to pass it on, then he can't get mad at us."

I called but Mark let it go to voicemail. I left a message that I had proof Lance wasn't one of the shifters who moved the body and that I had an update on the path they took. If I tried to fill in the details, I'd start rambling.

"Okay, you can tell Dolph whenever you want." I'd deal with Mark's disapproval later. I mean, I know I was dating him, but when he was on a case, it was like we were strangers.

"I'm off at midnight," he said. "Text me if Mark checks in. What was that about the path they took?"

I thought about what Pretty told me. "They saw the two shifters come past," I said. "Do you know how the search is going? Will it help to know they must have come from outside the village? On the path, maybe?"

"I'll pass it on to Dolph," he said. "He's keeping me out of the search. I thought it was because he didn't trust me, but now I think he does. He's left me to work with you all. Does that make sense?"

His confusion was apparent even without my powers; he'd remembered to block me again. Was the animosity between Lance and Dolph as bad as everyone seemed to think? Or had it just gone on because no one questioned it?

"You can ask him, right?" I said. "I don't know enough about anything to be sure, but he didn't expressly tell us to stay away.

He said his alpha seemed to want us to investigate, just couldn't ask outright. Like he was too proud.

16

Mark didn't call back. Lance didn't text me to say how his meeting with Dolph went. And over breakfast, Phillip assigned me a task to test my ability to search things out for clients. Not that I'd be doing that at the Inner Spell, but I didn't argue. It took me an hour to find three of the requested books online at one magical store in Toronto, and two mundane secondhand stores; one in Paris, one in Jakarta.

I made notes and went looking for Phillip.

"Make sure you do," he said to whoever was on the other end of the phone when I found him in the office. He ended the call and looked up at me.

I told him the results of my searches.

"Good work. And fast. Go ahead and order them with the bookstore account," he said. "Give them the house in Sechelt as a delivery address. I like to check over the merchandise before passing it to the client."

"Why would a mundane store have magical books?"

"It's unusual," he said. "And they are generally listed as fantasy or new age books. Sometimes a witch loses a copy.

The books just seem to find their way to wherever they need to be."

That was vague. I didn't push for details because I needed to head out. If Mark didn't call by the time Phillip was finished, I was going to look for him. And I'd always have time to ask lots of questions after we found the killer. Given time, I could actually narrow down the list to what I'd need for my business rather than a bookstore.

"Is there anything else?"

"Nothing new for you. Did you get your estimate for The Inner Spell?"

"Yes, but I haven't had a chance to look at it yet." Elias's email arrived overnight, and Phillip had sent me to do work before I could open it.

"You can make some changes if you want," he said. "I don't know what happens in the mundane world, but Elias won't gouge you. His estimate is lower than we expected."

Phillip was on the council and received the same email as me. "I don't have any experience with trades," I said. "We couldn't afford to buy a house, so no renovations or anything."

He turned away as though he was embarrassed my parents were poor. I didn't mean it to be a jab.

"I'll look at the details and get back to him today," I said. "He can get started as soon as I give the okay, right? The council doesn't have to meet?"

"Unless the costs start to rise beyond a reasonable amount, you're set to go." He looked back at me. "Take the rest of the day off."

I didn't need to be told twice. I ran upstairs and checked that I had a pocket full of food for any sources. My phone was fully charged and still nothing from Mark. Time to find out where he was.

I called Destroyer as I ran toward Mark's house.

"We have not found anything," Destroyer reported. "The shifters are getting in our way, but we persevere."

"Do you know where Mark is?"

"He is at home with the dog."

I thanked him and slowed as I approached Mark's door. I could hear Roy barking. Unless he spoke to me, I wouldn't know what he was saying. Instead of knocking on the front door, I ran around the back and rapped on the patio door.

Roy was definitely angry with Mark. They were facing each other. Mark was telling Roy to stop making so much noise. Roy was jumping up and barking.

"Hey," I called through the open slider. "Can I help?"

The noise stopped. Roy landed on all fours and turned to stare at me. "Nothing."

I looked at Mark. "He says it was nothing. It didn't sound like it."

"Well, it wasn't a big deal. We sometimes get into disagreements, but since I don't talk dog, I have no idea what the problem is. If he's not going to tell you, I guess it's over."

I glanced at Roy, who was eating, and I guess I had to take Mark's word. "Did you get my message?"

"I did, but you need to step back. This is too dangerous."

Why did he do that? Ask for my help and then as soon as I did, push me away? "Do you want the details?"

"Will you stop putting yourself in the middle of things?"

"I'm not willing to make any promises," I said.

"Fine." He pulled out his phone and set it to record. "Go ahead."

Had Dolph called him? I should have asked Lance before coming here. Too late now. I relayed all the information I had and waited for him to ask his questions.

"I'll get Dolph to redirect his pack to the path," he said.

"Destroyer is getting his bird army to search for a place with a lot of blood and damage," I said in the spirit of cooperation. "He hasn't found anything yet. Do you have any idea what happened? Why someone would want to kill her? And so brutally?"

Roy came over and sat beside me, staring at Mark. I patted his head and told him I was okay.

"He got a call," Roy said, "before you got here. Someone he doesn't like."

I gave him another pat. He wouldn't be able to give me anything more because of his binding to Mark.

"Did Dolph call?" I asked. I mean, who else would get him so riled up?

"No. Should I be expecting a call?"

It wasn't Dolph who had a hold over him. I read anger and some kind of conflict eating at him. Whoever got to him held considerable power over his job. That didn't jibe with what I'd been told about how Mark became the cop.

"Lance was going to tell him what I found. To clear his name. Didn't you tell Dolph what Joe and Al said?" That might explain why Lance was still running around free.

"I don't report to the alpha. He doesn't have a say in my investigations."

So the big deadline meant nothing?

"Lance didn't have a choice," I said. "He can't go behind the alpha's back."

"And you leaving me a vague voicemail was the only way to cover your butts?" There was the wave of mixed emotions again.

This was not what I expected. And it wasn't going to get any better. "If you'd phoned me back, you'd know."

17

A bit later in the day I headed out to get Beulah so I could continue my investigation. I checked with Destroyer, and he still had no news. How a crowd of carrion birds couldn't find a bloody murder scene, I don't know. I stopped stomping out my frustration. Magic! Of course there was something blocking the scent. Even if I hadn't asked them to search, without something to keep them away, the vultures would have found the site already. And so would everyone who was searching if they just looked up to see the carrion birds circling.

The idea that a spell was cast to cover the scent opened up my mind to all kinds of possibilities. Would it make sense to try to find a place on the island that had no scent? Or did spells have a scent? In the last case, the killer used pepper to discourage trackers. But no one mentioned it this time.

I sent a text to my friends. *What about a spell? To cover the odors? Can we track that?*

D and Lilibeth responded right away with a smiley emoji and a version of 'I'll check'.

Lance didn't respond. I told myself he was still with Dolph and there was no reason to worry, but I did. I turned toward the bike park to get Beulah for a ride out to the shifter village when my phone pinged with a text.

Not Lance. Mrs. Vestum. *Come to my home.*

No indication what she wanted to talk about, so I was left to compile a list in my head. Phillip said the budget for The Inner Spell was fine, but did that mean the other council members thought the same? Or had I accidentally crossed some line, and she was about to chastise me? Should I go alone? Should I ask Destroyer to come with me?

Destroyer! I hadn't passed on my idea about the spell.

When he answered my call and I told him my thoughts, he said, "So, look for a place that doesn't smell of carrion? That's most of the island."

"No, how about a spot that doesn't smell at all?"

"That is an idea worthy of a crow's familiar," he said. "I will pass on the instructions."

At least now I felt like I'd accomplished something. I headed to Jan's place and ordered coffee and some Danish to take to Mrs. V's. He gave me her favorites and wished me luck.

My path to her cottage went through a small copse of hazel trees. It amazed me every time I passed through trees and shrubs that shouldn't grow here. The earth witches kept a huge variety of flora going around the island.

"Hey." The voice came from one of the trees.

I looked over and saw a chipmunk staring at me from one of the branches. I guess the earth witches were looking after the fauna, too.

"Yeah, you, witch," he said.

"Do you want something?" I always carried food with

me for any animal, but my hands were full. "What's your name? And if I put this on the ground, is it safe?"

"Too many questions. Name is Wander. Don't want your human stuff."

I put the bag with the pastries on the path and reached into my pocket. "Okay, why did you call me over?"

"Why are you going to pay me if I'm the one asking?" This chipmunk had an attitude. I didn't let it get to me.

"Seems polite," I said.

"Why are the birds flying all around?"

I explained what Destroyer's army was doing.

"Makes us nervous," Wander said. "How would you like having your predators always in the corner of your eye?"

"We need to find the place where she was killed," I said. "Sorry it's upsetting. I hope it will get back to normal soon."

"What kind of thing are they trying to find?" Wander's eyes hadn't left the food in my hand.

"A place with a lot of damage, the fight would have been violent. And probably a lot of blood."

"We'll look, too. My family, maybe some like us. How do we tell you? How much food is it worth?"

They would use a lot of energy running around the island. I could be generous. "Who all will be looking?"

"Like us. Squirrels, voles, marmots, you name it. We see things no one else does. How much food?"

Okay, so I had food for all those kinds of animals. "Can any of you speak crow?"

"Some, but it's a scratchy language," Wander said.

"I live over the bookstore," I said. "You know where that is?"

"Yes. With the old witch. He's not as kind to us as you are. Thinks we eat his books."

"Do you?"

"Only if we are very hungry, but mice, yes. How do we tell you?"

"Just have someone talk to me," I said. "I'm mostly outside these days."

"Food?"

I dropped the whole handful of food beside the path. "I can set up something to pay for information."

"Trust you," Wander said. "We find. Not birds."

I thanked him, picked up my pastry bag and headed to the grouchy witch house. While I walked, I mulled over some way to set up a feeder for this whole crowd of informants.

18

M rs. V was making an effort. I felt her struggle not to snap at me when I arrived. The coffee and pastries helped make up for the fact that I hadn't dropped everything and rushed over as soon as I got the text. Although I hoped she didn't know I'd bought them to stall arriving.

She invited me into the kitchen and brought out mugs and plates. I guess drinking out of a cardboard cup wasn't on the list of things polite witches did. I waited quietly for her to transfer the coffee and treats to china. I wasn't about to open the discussion when I didn't know what she wanted from me.

"You are investigating this new death?"

No small talk today. Okay, that meant this would be short and sweet.

"We are, but Mark doesn't like it. As usual, he asked us to help, then he told me to back off."

I sipped my coffee and waited for her to continue. When I first arrived on Henbane, I thought she hated me. Then I learned she was protecting the island, and her meanness wasn't personal. I was still scared of her. And then, when she told me a few days ago that she didn't think the killings were my fault, I came to respect her. It didn't make her less mean, but I guess it made me more understanding.

"That boy needs a backbone," she said. "Have you found anything that links to your mother?"

She was sure my arrival woke some secret about what my mother did. Whether she was right or not, someone was trying hard to keep that secret.

"They all knew my mother," I said. "I guess my father too, but nothing more than that. I don't know where to look or who to ask. I guess Phillip was a friend to both of my parents, but he never talks about it. No one does."

The only piece of information I'd gleaned was they, or we, really, weren't exiled. That Mom and Dad ran. And maybe someone else was to blame but got away with it because my parents weren't around to defend themselves.

"That's one thing that worries me the most," she said. "People who try to tell you something and can't physically speak. That's powerful magic."

I had no idea what was powerful or not, and I'd never find out if people kept dying. "Does that mean only a few witches could cast the spell? Is the spell killing them? Or is it the effort to overcome it?"

"It depends," she said. "We don't know when it was cast, or why. There are spells that live on with little reinforcement until they are tested. The victim might not know it was done, or it could have been cast recently by someone who knew the killer. It could have been on the victims, too. As to whether the spell itself is lethal, we may never know."

"What can we do? Is there a counter spell?"

She stared at me for a few seconds before getting up and

retrieving a thick book from her living room. The title read, *Compendium of Spells of Control.*

"You should have your own copy. Did Phillip not give you a list of books to study? I am aware that your time is limited, but a few hours here and there with the right publications would make a difference."

I thought about the children's books he'd handed me on day one. She didn't mean those. "I guess he's trying not to overwhelm me," I said in his defense, although I don't know why I felt the need.

"Disappointing. Perhaps he is the wrong mentor," she said, flipping through the pages. "The council will discuss it at our next meeting."

All I could do was hope they didn't assign her as my mentor. "I'm sure he's doing what he thinks is best. I'll make sure I look for a copy of this one when I get back."

She looked up from the page, placing her finger on a line to keep her place. "Be sure you do. And I will compile a list for you regardless of what Phillip Raziel thinks is appropriate. How on earth does he think you will be able to run a business when you are vulnerable to the simplest spell work?"

"I've learned a few," I said. "This isn't really why you wanted to talk to me, right?"

She pursed her lips and closed the book. "I intend to help you with your investigation."

19

I thanked whatever force in the universe made sure I wasn't in mid sip when she made her announcement.

"To protect the island?" I asked, because that was her role, apparently. Not just Henbane, but what seemed like the entire magical world. Of course, it could be a way to justify any actions.

"Of course," she said, "and to make sure you and your little gang don't make things worse. And now, after our talk, I think I'll also take a stronger hand in your training."

I tried to picture Mrs. Vestum riding her bike along with us or tramping through the deep forest and couldn't. I pulled up my big girl pants and asked, "How? I mean, thanks for the help with my training, but how will you help with the investigation?"

"I have ways to research that others do not. I have friends outside Henbane, and I have lived a very long time. That brings some wisdom, Cossi."

Was that the first time she'd used my first name? And without that taint of disdain I usually sensed. Whatever she used to hide from my power wasn't strong enough to cover the protective wave that almost knocked me over.

"Of course it does," I said. "And you've known almost everyone here for their whole lives. What are you going to research?"

"People," she said. "As you suspect, that's my strength. Before you ask, I will not tell you who until I have some kind of proof they are involved."

My stomach was churning, partly with excitement over getting her as an ally, and partly with fear that adding more people to the unofficial investigation was going to push Mark to lock us up.

"What about Mark?" Maybe she had a hold over him that could protect us.

She gave me a little huff of impatience. "That boy is doing his job. If we find anything for him to act on, we will inform him immediately. I will not join in this habit of yours of going after killers." She got up and put the kettle on. "As I see it, he is stuck reacting to incidents. If we only deal with each individual crime, then we will never catch the witch behind it. And I am not prepared to wait until he or she runs out of victims."

I sat back and closed my eyes. Yes, I suspected someone was behind it. It would be willfully stupid not to see there were connections, no matter how tenuous. I hadn't thought we could find the puppet master. None of us had, no matter how much I tried to wish it into being.

"I agree," I said. "I think this all goes back to the night of my mother's mistake. And someone keeps warning Mark to keep us out of it."

She poured the water into the teapot and asked if I wanted a cup. "Just plain tea."

"I should be heading out soon," I said. "We still have to

solve this murder. And I can't help you with the hunt for whoever is driving the crime waves."

"Fair enough. You will text me with anything you find." It wasn't a request.

"Yes. I do have one question," I said.

"Do you need me to guess?" she asked, back to her crabby self.

"Do you know who was with my parents on that night?" No one really wanted to tell me anything, but maybe she would.

"I do and I don't, which is to say I know who your parents would trust to support them. There were others in attendance that I haven't identified yet. That's where I will start my research. But you were also there. Perhaps a seeking will reveal something."

I was there? "But I was a little kid. What would I remember?"

"Possibly nothing. But you were not a baby. If we run out of options, we will arrange a session with Peter Macy."

Was I ready to go on a drug-fueled trip through what could be a pivotal event in my life? I had no idea. "We can talk when the time comes," I said. "I should go see if any of my animals have found something. We need a clue."

"Yes, go along. I will begin my part of the investigation shortly."

Wait. I'd agreed we would share our findings with her, but she'd changed the subject right after. "And if you find anything?"

"I will inform you first, but I will not wait for permission to pass news to Mark."

I guess she still trusted him, even though she agreed someone was controlling him. "Great. I'll let the others know you're part of the team."

20

———

I didn't know exactly what I expected when I gave Lilibeth, D, and Lance the update, but it wasn't a collective sigh of relief. We were sitting on the stump circle at The Inner Spell trying to sort through the short list of facts we had for some meaning in the case.

"I was trying to figure out who we could ask," D said. "My research isn't helping much, and she's right, it's because we don't know the island like the old witches. I'll send her some help and access to databases."

"I didn't have much success. There are so many spells," Lilibeth said. "The really powerful ones aren't used much. I'm really worried that she thinks there's a huge conspiracy behind it."

Lance sent a text, then looked at us. "I let Dolph know Mrs. V is on the case. I don't care what Mark thinks. If a witch like her is working with us, Dolph should back off."

And if Dolph was the one behind it all, Lance might have put Mrs. V in danger.

His phone pinged. "She already told him, so it's good that we didn't try to hide it," Lance said.

"I also asked the animals to be on the lookout for where Aria was killed," I said. I passed on Destroyer's lack of progress as well. "I know we're supposed to be concentrating on this murder, but do any of you have a guess at who's pulling the strings?"

"On Mark?" D asked. "No, but it could be a compulsion spell. It's banned, but the ingredients aren't hard to gather."

"Or it could be more mundane," I said. "Someone has some leverage. But I meant behind all the killings."

"There are only a handful of witches who could use that kind of spell; one that kills people who try to tell a secret," D said. "And they would have to be originals, or one of their kids. Whatever it is, or whoever is wielding it, the spell has got to be one of the banned ones. We aren't taught them. Sure, we learn the easy compulsion spell, and there are plenty of other allowed ones that, if I wanted to, I could pull a big one together. Something like compelling someone to always bring me a pastry. But that's all."

"I guess we leave it to Mrs. V," I said. "She's an original, right?"

"Yes," Lilibeth said. "You do trust her, right? I mean, she's the protector."

"I trust her," I said. I tried to ignore the little voice that said, 'she's able to block your power longer and more completely than others, and who knows what protecting the island might allow her to rationalize.'

Lance was still looking at his phone. "Dolph wants to know why his yard is overrun with vermin."

"Tell him not to hurt them," I blurted out. "Investigating. They're doing their best to figure out where Aria was killed."

Lance sent the text. "He would prefer not to have a horde of mice and squirrels arguing in his proximity, but he will leave them."

The image of an argument in the high squeak voices made me smile. "Let's hope they found something and are arguing over who tells me and gets fed."

"Maybe we should go over and find out?" Lilibeth said.

"She wasn't killed there," I said.

"Look up," Destroyer cawed at me. He flew low over my head and dropped a mouse on my shoulder. "News."

"Many news," the mouse said. "Take food to the entrance to dog people village, we will share."

I held up my hand so he could skitter down to my palm. "As soon as I can. What news?"

"Boss dog man is mean. Two paths from body place. More seeing from the night of the body. Same two dog men. Said more when they left. Said now he will have to deal with it. Not good for him to leave her to rot. Squirrels are bossy and greedy. I was scared of being eaten but flying was fun. I will run home. Boss dog man talked to the body-carrying dog men. Crow told birds the path to follow to find death place. Boss dog man yelled at us."

He stopped talking and stared at me.

"Is that it?" I repeated it like a translator as he spoke so the others understood. And D was recording.

"Yes."

"I can call Destroyer to fly you back."

He jumped in my hand like I'd shouted 'boo'.

"I will run. Flying is for stupid birds."

I knelt to let him leave.

"Okay," Lilibeth said. "That was weird. A lot of commentary, but I think there were some good clues."

D played back the recording while I took notes on my phone.

"Interesting that I only understand him in real life." Something to remember in the future.

"What he said about the shifters," Lance said, "it's not proof. I get that they wouldn't like Dolph, but it doesn't mean he would kill a member of the pack."

I read over the notes. While I listened to my informant, I'd tried not to get sidetracked with interpretation. Now that I had read the facts, it was easy to interpret as a list of reasons that blamed the Alpha.

"Two paths from body place. More seeing from the night of the body. Same two dog men. Said more when they left. Said now he will have to deal with it. Not good for him to leave her to rot. Boss dog man talked to the body-carrying dog men. Crow told birds the path to follow to find death place." I read the relevant points.

"Okay, it looks really bad that Dolph talked to the shifters who brought the body to him," Lance said.

"And he didn't mention it," Lilibeth said. "You think Mark is aware?"

21

"Dolph's under no obligation to tell us anything," I said. "Mark won't tell us if he knows. And I think we need to flesh this out before we take what we know to anyone."

"Mrs. V should know," D said.

"She might tell Mark," Lance said.

I held up my hand to stop the escalation into a full-on argument. "I agreed with her that we wouldn't keep secrets. I'll send her the entire text in case some of the tangents mean something to her. I'll tell her we think it's too flimsy to share and ask her if she agrees."

My preference was to keep it all between the four of us. Bringing Mrs. Vestum into the mix was new and a risk. That said, I was not going to go against my agreement with her for three reasons: I didn't break my word easily, she might have an insight, and the most important point, I was afraid of what she would do if I went behind her back.

I sent her the notes file and waited for her to respond. I posed the two conditions as questions so she would answer them.

"While we wait," Lance said, "I think we can figure out a bunch of legitimate reasons Dolph isn't involved."

"Don't be blind to the idea he can be the killer," Lilibeth said.

"Lance is right," I said. "This is all filtered through the mind of a rodent. We don't know who else saw them that night. We don't know why Dolph met with the two shifters, or what was said."

D looked up from his laptop. "You don't usually question the information from your animals."

"Because it's usually not secondhand," I said. "And we see the world differently than the animals around us. Are you updating the spreadsheet, D?"

"The points we think are important and then our thoughts. I've sent Mrs. V a link so she can participate."

She still hadn't answered. "Will she know how to open the attachment?"

D finished typing and closed his laptop. "I gave her a printed instruction sheet for most of the usual actions, so if she remembers, yes. But she does know how to text."

I guess he wasn't planning on entering our ideas as we talked. I pulled up the notes again and gave it a moment's thought.

"Wait," Lance said. "Someone's coming."

Was Mrs. V on her way to chastise us? Or Mark? She hadn't responded because she'd already forwarded the document to him?

Elias biked into sight with another witch behind him.

"I didn't expect you to be here," he said as he dismounted. "This is Janet. She's the expert in electrical and plumbing."

I shook hands with Janet and asked if he was going to start working.

"Just a walkthrough today," Janet responded for him.

"Bringing supplies on site tomorrow. You planning to hang out here? It's dangerous when I'm building."

"We'll find somewhere else," I said. "If I need to visit, I'll let you know."

"We'll leave you to it," Lance said before I could say pretty much the same thing. He turned to us to say, "We can go to my place."

That was a solid option. We'd be in the shifter village if anyone had more news. And if we really needed to talk to Dolph, he was a few steps away.

Mrs. V finally responded to my text. *I agree, but do not keep anything from me.*

I told Lilibeth, Lance, and D what she'd said. "I have an idea," I added, because something popped into my mind with her response. "What if we make her our liaison with Mark? A buffer."

"You think he'll be less likely to stop us if he doesn't hear from us?" Lilibeth asked quietly as we took our bikes from the side of a chalet.

"We can always hope. I'll be back in a second," I said. Grabbing my bike made me think about the clients who'd come to The Inner Spell. I found Elias in the farthest chalet talking to Janet.

"I'll need something to hold people's bikes," I said. "I can't remember if it's in the plan."

He gave Janet a look that I read as 'people are so annoying' and then did his magic to reveal the end result of my plans again. "Here," he said, pointing. "One space as a loading zone for supplies behind the barracks. Each chalet has a mount on the side for two bikes. Is that enough?"

"Sorry, I shouldn't have questioned you," I said, my focus held on the image of my dream business.

"He's just a grump," Janet said, giving Elias a playful slap on the arm. "None of his clients can remember everything about their projects. All of them ask what he thinks are stupid questions."

"I'm sorry anyway," I said. "I'll check what you wrote before I ask another one."

"That will save time," he said. "I'm waiting for some supplies. They'll be here next week. You need to go through everything in case you want to keep bits and pieces. I'll be getting rid of any loose things lying around."

I almost told him to go ahead because I'd looked around, and then I realized I hadn't. My searches were all about the Macy murder. I'd barely gone into any of the other buildings.

I told him I'd do it before the weekend, then went to join D and Lilibeth at the entrance to the path.

"Lance went ahead to make sure his place is ready," Lilibeth said. "And, I'm guessing, to pick up refreshments."

22

Two hours later, we ground to a halt in our search for meaning.

"We need to talk to Dolph," I said. "The only real thing that points to him is that he talked to the two people who moved the body. It could be just everyday pack business. The 'he' who has to deal with it might not be Dolph or the killer. Now that the body was found, the killer will have to deal with it, whatever it turns out to be."

"Someone wants in," Lilibeth said.

The lack of space inside Lance's home meant we were perched on different surfaces, Lilibeth closest to the door.

I heard a scratching noise as soon as we stopped talking.

"I hope your animals don't make a habit of using my place as a meeting point," Lance said as he reached across to push the door open.

A raccoon sprawled on the ground, a piece of paper clasped in her right hand.

"Sorry," I said as I hurried down to help her up.

"Door opened on me," she said woozily.

There wasn't room for the door to open inside, so I couldn't say more than sorry again. "Why did you come?"

"Crow told me. We were all searching around to find clues for food. Last time you paid for papers. I have papers."

"Lance, do you have anything special?" I could pay the usual way, but I'd emptied my supplies when we entered the shifter village as ordered by the mouse.

He moved to the tiny kitchen. "Eggs, some apples, not much other than what we just ate."

The raccoon's eyes widened at the promise of eggs.

"How many of you need to be paid?"

"Three raccoons one egg each," she said. "I get them you put eggs on ground."

"Wait, the paper?" I reached for it, but she pulled it away.

"When we have eggs." She ran off—well, waddled at speed was more accurate.

"Tell your familiar about the door," Lilibeth said. "I don't want to be acting doctor to any animal that comes by."

"Let them learn," Destroyer said when I thought at him.

"Eggs now." The raccoon was back with two buddies.

Lance came out and placed the payment on a clump of grass to the side of the house. "They are cold," he said.

"Not a problem," my source said as she tossed the scrap of paper toward me. "Bye."

I glanced around just in case another informant was headed our way, but the path was clear.

"So, what cost me my breakfast?" Lance asked.

I flattened the evidence on my lap. It was torn from a notebook. About half of the sheet was missing but the words on what I had were definitely worth buying Lance a new breakfast protein.

You know I saw you.

I have proof.

Pay or I tell everyone.

You have unti

The rest of the statement was on the missing part of the sheet.

"Blackmail?" Lance asked. "We should have asked your friend questions. Where was it found?"

Knowing someone was being blackmailed was useless until we figured out who the people involved were, or what happened to make someone vulnerable to extortion. I didn't even know what would be so bad someone would pay or kill to keep it secret.

"Maybe Destroyer knows," I said. I thought at him.

"Behind the alpha's home. Raccoons like garbage, remember. In his compost pile. I may have more news soon."

I didn't want to tell them. If it was in Dolph's compost, it didn't mean it was his, right? Anyone could have tossed something there. If Dolph was being blackmailed, he would have burned the evidence.

I told them.

"Not possible," Lance said. "Dolph doesn't answer to anyone."

"You know someone is behind everything that's been happening," Lilibeth said.

"A shifter would never dare," Lance said. I felt the outrage he was desperately trying to suppress.

"The blackmailer could be a witch," D said. "Or it could be the person being blackmailed came to Dolph for help. The note was tossed into the compost without thinking."

"If you put it in the database, Mrs. V will tell Mark," Lilibeth said.

"I think we need to talk to Dolph," I said. "If it's so

unlikely he could be the blackmailee, he should be happy to tell us."

"It's not going to help our relationship," Lance said.

"If you aren't there, it will be worse," Lilibeth said. "You have to deal with it eventually."

There was that hint she knew why Dolph was the alpha again. I didn't ask because this wasn't the time to satisfy my nosiness.

"I'll do it," I said. "In person. I'll tell him you all know, but I won't let him know Mrs. Vestum is part of the team. She isn't really working on Aria's murder, anyway."

"What will you say?" Lance asked.

"I'll play the newbie card," I said. "He can't accuse me of being offensive when I don't know the rules. I'll say we found the note and show him a picture of it."

"So he can't take the original?" D asked. "Good idea, we can pass that along to Mark."

"Can I just text him, or should I go over there and knock on the door?" Now that it was decided, I wanted to get the whole thing over with.

"Text him," Lance said, handing me his phone to read the number. "I'm not sure you want to just spring this on him."

Dolph responded that he couldn't meet for a couple of hours.

"That doesn't help at all," I said after showing them my screen. "I can't hold back on telling Mark for too long."

"A couple of hours won't make a difference," D said. "Maybe something else will turn up while you're waiting."

My phone pinged, and despite my hope it was the Alpha changing his mind, Elias's name showed on the caller ID. *Need answers, can you come to the site right now?*

23

A t least it was something to fill my time while I waited for Dolph to be available. D and Lilibeth rode with me to where the path split between the village and farther into the island. I watched them go, D to do more research and Lilibeth to take care of her animals and look up spells.

When I got to The Inner Spell, Elias was sitting on one of the log seats, making notes on his pad and drinking from a thermos. He nodded to me as I placed Beulah against the first chalet. Nothing seemed different to me. What kind of answers did he need?

"Last details," he said. "And something we found."

I joined him. "Is there a way we can make these more like seats?" I asked. "It feels like a great place to talk after a day of experimenting or whatever my clients are doing."

"Already on the list," he said. "You need to choose the fittings so I can order them."

I thought he'd already told me everything was ordered. "Will it delay us?" I didn't know how to feel if the answer was yes. A few more days would give me a chance to get some marketing underway, but weeks meant I wouldn't be able to open this year.

"Unless you want some rare items, no. But I thought you were going rustic, so I've pulled together some choices."

He could have done this over text. Why did he make me come all the way up here? Was it something to do with the case? I stomped on the paranoia train building in my head. Not everything was a clue or a plot to get in our way.

He showed me options that covered decor from plain black metal to brushed nickel. Each chalet would have a small washroom behind a partition so the occupant didn't need to use a shared washroom. The list included those items and shelving brackets, fire grates and door handles. The prices were similar, and I hadn't planned to go with gold fixtures anyway.

"Is there some kind of cultural or magical property I need to know about?" I'd feel like a complete idiot if I put in something that caused some magical feng shui disaster.

He looked at me for a long moment, and I wondered if just asking the question was wrong.

"I forget you don't have history. You look so much like your mother; it feels like I know you."

Looking like Mom should make me feel great. She was a wonderful mother and pretty when she wasn't bent over some recipe or digging in the garden. But it came with such a weight of mystery I couldn't quite enjoy it. Or suspecting she was responsible for all these murders made it hard to think of her as a good person.

"People have mentioned that before. Did you know her well?" I had given up on assuming age for witches. He could be Mom and Dad's friend from childhood, or someone who taught them in school.

"She was kind to all of us," he said. "Some witches are

kind of snooty. But your parents didn't care what people did, just that they were kind and honest."

"It's a change to hear something that isn't about her mistake," I said. I took his pad from him to give me a chance to sort out my emotions before I said anything more or burst into tears.

"Don't you listen to that gossip," Elias said. "No one knows what happened but the people who were there."

"Do you know who was there?" That was a key piece of information to solve who might be behind all the murders.

"They kept it quiet. Who's going to admit they were part of that disaster?"

True, but eventually Mrs. V and I would ferret them out.

"So is one of these styles better for meditation, or experimentation?"

"The black is centering. The brass is purifying, and the nickel is good luck." He took the pad back.

I wanted all of that, but it would look awful to have that mix in each chalet. "In the new building, I think nickel would be best. Half the chalets in the black and the other half in brass. Will that be okay?"

He was filling out the order form, so I didn't get an answer right away. It gave my mind too much time to wander around all my problems. I wasn't ready to open The Inner Spell. I didn't have a place to live other than Phillip's apartment. I had to face Dolph with an accusation — it wasn't, but that's how he'd see it.

"Okay. I'll be picking everything up on Monday morning in Sechelt," Elias said, breaking my anxiety spiral. "The wood and furniture will arrive over the next few days. We'll be done about two weeks before the summer festival."

I'd forgotten about that, and my date with D. "I don't know when that is," I said, "or what it is, really."

"We celebrate the equinox. Lots of power in the season change," he said. "You can get more information from one of your friends, or Phillip. I don't have time to educate you."

Since I wanted to get my business up and running quickly, I let that go. "You said you had something to show me?"

He stood and started walking toward the barracks — now I needed a name for that because 'barracks' sounded too much like a military site. "First, I'll show you where we found it."

24

I followed him to the edge of the forest, where the far wall of my main building would be. He stopped by the side of a large fir.

"Janet and I were looking at the ground quality for drainage. Need a trench here so you won't get flooded every time it rains."

He pointed to a hole in the ground, like a core sample. It made sense to me that they would need to investigate the ground conditions, but I didn't see anything beyond the test. Was I supposed to recognize some kind of imminent disaster?

"Okay. So, is everything good with the ground?"

He rolled his eyes at me like I was nuts. That's when I realized I couldn't read him. Not like his emotions were shielded, but like he didn't have any. That was impossible; living people felt things no matter what kind of witch they were. Or non-witch, for that matter. There was no way I could ask him without giving offense. Like asking if he was a zombie or a vampire. There were books at Phillip's place I could check. I also didn't want to ask my friends because I didn't like bringing up my power to read emotions. And maybe I didn't want to learn there were undead living on the island.

"No. We don't need a hole that large. We kept digging around something. A box. It's locked, but since this is your property, it's now yours."

The hole was about big enough to hold a shoe box. Whatever it contained, it wasn't a house or a car. "Where is it?"

He walked back to the chalets and opened the door to the first one. This was the one where Mrs. Macy's body was found. By me. I still needed to do some kind of cleansing, but that could wait until everything was built. The last time I was inside, it was empty. Now there were five boxes in the pit, and a couple of toolboxes on the ground in the back.

"We took all the things we found and put them here for you. Janet is getting ready to start her work, so she needed the space."

"All of this was in the chalets?" I would need to borrow one of the bike trailers to get it home.

"Yes, and unless something else is buried, this is all that's left. You need to take it away before we start."

If only I had all the time in the world. "Some of this might belong to the earth witches," I said. "They've been using the chalets. I guess I can put out a message to come to my place to pick up what they want."

He didn't respond.

"Okay, I'll clear it out as soon as I get time. Is anything really heavy?" I didn't want to find out I needed help at the last minute. The way this week was going, I'd be here past midnight.

"No. Tell me when you're done. Maybe I can start early. I have to go now. Finishing up a job." He looked at the contents of the pit. "Some of that is pretty old, so be careful not to break anything. The box we found is the black one."

He left before I could thank him, or ask him anything more, or, I don't know, find some way to figure out where his emotions were.

I sent a text to the gang to let them know I was done at The Inner Spell. Then, Dolph told me he was ready to meet. I replied that I was on my way and pushed back at all the anxiety I carried for telling the alpha we thought he was being blackmailed, and that he might be the killer, or he was being framed.

I made a note to stop by and get one of the trailers to bring everything back to my room.

25

My nerves didn't settle on the ride, or on the walk through the shifter village. All the stupid books I'd read involving alphas raced through my brain. Would he fly into a rage? Would he lash out and blame Lance?

I stood looking at his house for a moment while I struggled to find a non-accusatory way of bringing up what we found. I had no idea if he lived in what was essentially the house assigned to the alpha, or if this was his house regardless of title. It was set apart from the other houses. On an island formed by the road that split around it. Like he was protecting himself from casual contact.

The front door opened and he stepped out, glaring at me. It didn't matter that he looked like a blond god, all shifters were gorgeous. His annoyance floated across to me. I guess he didn't feel the need to block my power.

"What are you waiting for, witch?"

I shrugged and marched across the street and past him, through the door. "Let's get this over with."

He smiled. "Fine. Tea? Beer?"

"Water would be nice." All this riding around left me parched.

He led me into the kitchen. This time the whiteness didn't feel cold, but it wrapped me in a clean and safe vibe. Weird. Was I being manipulated by a spell? Like when people baked cookies to make their home more appealing to a buyer.

I pulled out my phone while he filled a glass. The picture of the note was the last one I took, so it would be easy to access when I was ready. But now that I was here, I couldn't quite figure out how to start. Just a bold 'are you being blackmailed?' seemed too harsh. I wanted a conversation, not a fight about accusations.

He placed the glass on the counter and pulled out a stool for me. Was this a shifter thing? Making people comfortable in your home? Like he was acting automatically? I could still feel the annoyance behind a sheen of curiosity.

"Before you tell me why you wanted to see me," he said, pulling out a stool for himself, "I want to talk to you about investigating Aria's murder."

That was the last thing I expected. He was on the council and never seemed to like or respect me. To be honest, he'd basically ignored me. "Isn't Mark doing a good job?" Or was he about to warn me off the case?

He focused on wiping at some nonexistent crumbs from the countertop. "He is. I am not sure he can do what is needed."

I opened my mouth to ask what exactly he meant but he waved me to silence. "He is competent. I know you are involved with him, no need to defend a potential mate."

My entire body burned with embarrassment, and some anger. Who was he to determine my personal life?

"We went out twice," I said. "What did you mean that he's not able to do what is needed?"

He grinned at me as if my reaction was a joke. I gripped my phone to remind myself I had some ammunition in this fight.

"He is restrained by certain oaths, and perhaps other pressures," he said. "You have had success with investigations. You are new here and have no... entanglements."

So he thought Mark was being controlled too, or I just read that into his comments. "I'm not an investigator."

"Recent history shows that to be untrue."

I couldn't argue that point. "So you want me to find the killer? What if you don't like the results?"

"The truth is the truth, no matter what we like or hate."

"And Mark? Have you told him you're asking me, us, to do his job?"

"Are you hungry?"

He didn't wait for an answer. Grabbing a plate from a cupboard, he cut an apple and some cheese. By the time the food was settled in front of me, he'd lost the underlying emotions and I realized he thought I'd said yes.

"You solved the other two murders without his permission. I think it would be better if we didn't make this arrangement formal. Will you and your friends, and your animals, find whoever killed Aria and bring them to justice?"

"Are you being blackmailed?" I asked. Time for me to take some control. "We found this note in your compost."

He glanced at the phone I held out. "You were digging in my compost? That's dedication."

I didn't miss the fact he hadn't answered the question.

"Not me, my animals. So?"

He read the note and went to the cupboard under his

sink. He brought out a bundle wrapped in paper. "I am not," he said. "This is my compost." He opened the package to show me a pile of vegetable peelings. "As you can see, I do not include paper other than the wrapping."

I wrapped the paper again and pushed it toward him. "That doesn't really prove anything."

"I am not being blackmailed," he said again. "Ask your informant if there were other notes in the compost."

I guess if I was investigating a murder, proving blackmail might just be part of narrowing down the suspects.

"I will. If it's not you, who might be trying to frame you?"

"No one. Perhaps this blackmailer discarded his or her note coincidently in my pile. Or it blew in."

"Before I agree to investigate, I need a few answers," I said. Of course I was going to continue on the case. Having Dolph not actually helping but at least staying out of the way would be valuable.

"It wasn't a question," he said. "What do you wish me to say?"

I had to believe he didn't know how manipulative he sounded. I wanted real answers I could count on, not him telling me what I wanted to hear. If I went back to Lilibeth, D, and especially Lance, I needed to be very sure it was a good idea.

"When you say 'bring the killer to justice', what do you mean?"

He grinned again and I should have felt something more than exasperation. It was a charming smile, but I think I'd just had a few too many charming smiles that covered creepy behaviors in my dating past.

As if he realized the usual tactic wasn't working, he

turned serious. "That Mark takes him or her into custody and the council decides the punishment."

"Not that you take out some kind of shifter vengeance?"

"If you had grown up on Henbane, you would know how offensive that was," he said.

"Not my choice, so I'm happy to hear your story."

"Shifters elsewhere may live by a wilder code, but when my ancestors requested sanctuary here, they swore an oath that binds all generations who stay. We abide by the laws of the island. So, the murderer will be treated just like the ones before. I will not interfere. I will not take offense, even should Lance Volk question me. You are free to conduct your investigation as you think best."

I heard the unspoken words, '*until I decide otherwise.*'

"I will ask about the note," I said. I hoped I wasn't about to get a list of the compost components and the state of decay from my raccoon friend. "Let's say you are telling the truth about it not being about you."

He actually growled. I lifted an eyebrow. He'd literally just said he wouldn't or couldn't take offense.

"I didn't say I would like it," he said.

"Fine. I know what a human could be blackmailed for, but what about a shifter? There's definitely something going on."

He pricked his ears. Yes, I know he shouldn't be able to do that, it's a canine thing, but the way he tilted his head gave me the impression he'd heard something unexpected.

"Your crow is near," he said.

"Don't worry about him," I said. "He'll interrupt if he thinks it's important."

"I suppose your answer is fairly simple. Much like mundane humans and witches, shifters don't like their secrets exposed. The victim may have mated with an inappropriate partner. Or maybe collecting something no one would approve of. Or perhaps a lie told in the past is coming to light."

"What would be an inappropriate mate?" I thought everyone on Henbane was pretty cool about sex.

"Someone they have been banned from mating with," he said. I must have looked shocked because he gave me that grin again. "Because of inbreeding, Cossi, not possession. Shifters are less affected by breeding within families, but still, we have our human side. We are a small population here, so we have to be careful. We choose mates off-island. Some come to live here, some leave to join a new pack. It's healthy."

It carried a giant ick factor, but I understood the need. "So to keep a secret, the shifter could move away?"

"Yes, but this is our home. We don't leave on a whim."

That meant our suspect pool just expanded from the relatively manageable number of Henbane Islanders to the entire paranormal population. "Has anyone left or returned lately?"

"Two that I know about. There could be more. I am supposed to be informed, but perhaps someone has a good reason to delay. Do you think it likely that a blackmailer or a murderer will follow the pack's rules? Or the island's?"

"You never know. Who are the two?" I needed to get the information in the database, and find out if Mrs. V knew more about potential blackmail victims.

"I'm surprised Lance didn't mention his aunt returned; Stella Volk. And Kris Tamaska. He left long ago to pursue some research. I have no idea what. Things were a little chaotic at the time."

Long ago could be a hundred years or two years. I made

note of the names and tried to silence the suspicion that Lance was keeping information from us.

"Before you ask," he continued, "I have no idea if they are possible blackmailers, killers, or victims. I regret I have neglected to keep my mind on the minutia of the pack members' lives."

Destroyer was waiting for me on the front porch. "You survived," he said.

"He's not going to eat me," I said. "Did you find anything? Because I have to talk to my friends."

"No. It's night, we are sleeping now, and the creatures who run in the dark will take over. Do not be afraid if one comes to find you."

He could have thought that at me. "Why are you here in person?"

"What if you needed my help in dealing with the alpha? I am supreme bird alpha now, so I have status with him."

If he kept claiming titles, I might be dealing with crow emperor soon. If it made him happy, I didn't care. "I'm fine. Did you hear what he said?"

"No."

Something he wasn't the king of. I had no idea such a thing existed.

"I need to talk to the raccoon again," I said. "You know which one?"

"I will find her before she sleeps tomorrow morning,"

Destroyer promised, sounding exactly like he was planning a world-shaking campaign.

"Dolph says the note wasn't for him, so I need a lot more details. Will he remember in the morning?"

"It doesn't matter, I cannot find him now. I will spend the night here in the village. If anything happens, I will know immediately. Now leave me before I fall asleep on the ground where I might get trampled."

I left him to it. We weren't going to get far tonight anyway, so receiving the information in the morning would be fine. I was at the point where I needed a nap soon. Or a full night's sleep, but a nap would be better than nothing.

I sent a text to the group, not including Mrs. V because I kept forgetting to add her, and I still got a little fizz of fear when I thought about her.

I got the reply from Lance immediately. *We're at D's.*

Close to home, and I might get some sleep after the update.

I parked Beulah in her space and walked to D's from there. He greeted me with a hot chocolate and cookies at the door.

"Come on in."

I appreciated the treat and kicked off my shoes. In the living room, I found the reason for the bribe. Not only Lance and Lilibeth, but Mrs. Vestum sat waiting for me. Crap.

"Add me to this text group now, Cossi," she demanded.

I put the hot chocolate and cookies on the coffee table and pulled out my phone. I already had her in my contacts, so it was just a matter of seconds before I gave up my chance at keeping secrets from her. I knew I could have started a separate list for us, but someone had invited her to this meeting, so I figured I wouldn't be able to hide it.

I told them about my discussion with Dolph. "We

should be able to work without interference. At least from him. Mark is another matter."

"He will keep his word," Mrs. Vestum said, "or I will deal with the alpha. Mark hasn't been a problem in the past. I assume you know how to handle him."

I tried to find some kind of hidden meaning in her words, but I couldn't. It seemed like she'd committed to us, at least for this case. I could only hope this was the last time we would be digging into crimes.

"Lance, did you know your aunt was on the island?" I asked. Before we went any further, I had to get that cleared up. If he'd kept that a secret, we'd have to put him on the suspect list and lose him as part of the team.

"No. I'm surprised she came back. But that's her right. I guess I should find her when we're done and welcome her."

"Let her come to you, boy," Mrs. Vestum said. "You don't owe her anything. And before you say Dolph will demand it, he hasn't yet."

The others seemed to believe him, so I did too. "And this other person, Kris Tamaska?"

"Let me look into him," Mrs. Vestum said. "I remember he was around when your parents left, Cossi. In fact, now you mention him, I'd forgotten your family wasn't the only one to flee around that time."

"You think he might be the killer?" I'm not sure why it seemed easier if a virtual stranger murdered Aria.

"I said let me look into it," Mrs. V repeated.

"Raccoon is coming," Destroyer said in my mind. I don't know if crows yawned, but that's what it sounded like.

I let the others know. "Maybe we can get Dolph off our suspect list."

"I'll leave the door open," D said. "We have things to talk about that you don't know."

I tried to remember what everyone was doing while I met with Elias and then Dolph. Looking for the path to the place Aria died and researching a bunch of stuff.

"Lance and I followed the directions you got from your sources," Lilibeth said. "We didn't find what we needed, but there's something weird. You tell her, Lance."

He paused to take a sheet of paper from the floor. A map

"Here's where we looked," he said, pointing to shaded areas. "The trail was clear at Dolph's place when you know what to look for. We were initially trying to find blood and follow the scent. I decided to try something simpler. Broken leaves, footprints, that kind of thing."

"And?" The shaded parts were kind of blobs scattered around the island. "Are those areas cleared, so we can send animals and shifters to look at the rest of the island?"

He shook his head. "No. Those areas are—I guess the best way to say it is they don't seem to exist. I mean they do, there's no hole in the island, but any time someone tries to go in there, they end up in a different part of Henbane altogether."

I checked the map again. Each shaded space was off the normal paths. They didn't correspond with where other people were killed. Or someone's territory, or anything I could think of. "I'll get Destroyer to see if the animals and birds can go in."

I think he would have mentioned blank spaces, and I had no idea how to direct him, but it was the best I could do.

"Is there a spell we could try to counter?" I asked.

"Not that I've been able to find," D said.

"I don't remember any such spell, nor can I think of a reason to create one." Mrs. Vestum's voice shook with fear.

28

I f someone was able to hide parts of the island, what else would they be able to do?

"Is this the secret experiment Jeffery Peak was doing?" I asked. In our last case, Jeffery was framed for the murder of his friend, and a spell wiped his memory. They'd been working on some new discovery, but he'd forgotten the details.

"He hasn't remembered yet," Mrs. V said. "I will contact him in the morning. We need to know a great deal more about this absence regardless of what Mr. Peak does or doesn't know. Finding out what exactly exists and does not in these spaces is vital. Can magic be done? Can we restore it?"

I wanted to give her a hug. Something was threatening the whole way of life she was bound to protect. But I didn't want to be turned into a toad.

"Your friend is almost here," Lance announced.

"Who?" I asked.

"The raccoon. I assume it is the same one that your familiar sent. Perhaps we will get our answers."

I hadn't much thought of the animals as my friends, but I guess he had a point.

I went to the door to look for her and almost jumped out of my skin when she hopped onto the top step from the shadows. She let out a squeak of surprise.

"Come in," I said when I got my breath back.

She waddled ahead of me into the living room and came to a stop. "Many people."

I stepped around her and looked for a place to make her comfortable. "They won't hurt you," I said. "What's your name?"

She looked up at me and said, "Grabber. I am the mate of Shover. Stop calling me a female in your head."

I made the introductions and offered him a cushion to sit on. "We have a few questions."

"Ask one," Grabber said. "Too many and I will forget."

Raccoons were really helpful before, when we were looking for Jeffery. They could get into a lot of places and follow instructions. They did tend to get distracted if given too many options.

"Are you the raccoon who brought us the paper from the alpha's compost?" I didn't know enough about them to know for sure, but I'd have sworn that one was female.

"My mate. I was there. I sent her to give it to you."

"There are two things we want to know," I said after translating for the others in the room. "The first one was about the compost heap. The alpha says it is not normal for him to put paper in there."

"Only that paper was there," Grabber said. "On top. Easy to find."

So someone had dropped it there. On purpose or by accident? "Is there a way for you to know who touched it?"

"Smelled like witch. I don't know who. But not dog man."

I passed that on.

"In that case, I may be able to track the owner," Mrs. V said. "Do you have the original scrap?"

I dug it out of my pack. I'd have to give it to Mark tomorrow, but Mrs. V could do what she needed to in the meantime.

"I guess knowing who touched it last will be useful. Either the blackmailer, or the victim," D said. "Or, and here's a weird idea: maybe someone was planning to extort someone but changed their mind."

Not a weird idea at all. We'd assumed the blackmail happened, and it resulted somehow in Aria's murder. Maybe D was right, and even if he wasn't, the note could have nothing to do with the killing.

"What is second thing?" Grabber asked. "I have hunting to do before the sun comes up."

"We'll pay you in food," I said. "Something you can take back to your family."

D went into the kitchen and returned with a bundle small enough for Grabber to carry. "Fruit and meat," he said.

He looked at the package and sniffed the air. "Good."

"Can you read a map?" I asked, holding up the drawing of the island with the shaded areas.

"If that is map, no."

"He needs landmarks or something," I said.

Mrs. Vestum took the map and traced her finger along the closest path. She made thinking noises for a minute and then turned to Grabber.

"In this place was the dam the beavers built. Do you know that?"

Grabber nodded, his eyes focused on the bundle of food. "Still is there. Beavers too. Why?"

Mrs. V glanced at me and frowned to indicate I should take over.

"The shifters can't follow any traces into this or the other areas. For them it's like the place does not exist. And when anyone goes in, they end up somewhere else."

"I don't know about that," Grabber said. "You want us to try to go in?"

That seemed a big ask. It was one thing for a shifter or a witch to make their way back if they ended up some other place on the island. A raccoon? Most of the animals I talked to were too small to range far.

"We'll see what the birds find first," I said after checking with the others. "Thank you."

Grabber wrapped his hands around the handle D had fashioned with the string and waddled to the door. "No thanks, food is good."

29

We decided to wrap it up for the night after Grabber left. I was exhausted, and I could tell the others weren't far behind. Lance decided staying with D was a good idea until we could talk to Dolph. Mrs. V was already aching to start her research and find a way to stop her island disappearing. Lilibeth walked with me until we got to her place, across the street from my home.

"We need to be really careful, Cossi," she'd said before we separated. "Something that has Mrs. Vestum worried is going to be really serious."

"We'll help her," I said. "This is our home too."

We said goodnight, and as much as I wanted to crawl into bed, I remembered the boxes at the Inner Spell. It wouldn't even take an hour. I grabbed Beulah and a trailer and headed for the chalets.

By the time I headed upstairs to my room, the apartment was dark, not surprising since it must have been around two AM when I slipped inside. I was relieved when I didn't have to face Phillip with all the secrets I was hoarding.

. . .

I DIDN'T HAVE a great sleep because as soon as I laid down and closed my eyes, the thought that these blank spaces were a result of my mother's mistake popped into my head.

I grabbed a muffin from the plate Phillip left in the kitchen. He was always experimenting with new mixes, some not so great, some delicious enough that he gave the recipe to Jan and Zoe to sell in their cafes. This morning's was a little too earthy for me, but I needed sustenance.

We'd agreed to meet at Lance's place in the morning. I could ask the mice if anything happened, and then all of us, except Mrs. V, would go talk to Dolph.

I was the last one to arrive. No one, including the mice, had anything to report. "Okay, is Dolph expecting us?"

"I told him we were on our way," Lance said. "Did Destroyer agree to investigate the blanks?"

So now we'd made a name for the shaded areas. Places that shouldn't exist didn't deserve names, but we needed to call them something. It just gave me a sense we were giving them power by naming them.

"He's on it. None of the birds noticed anything, but he thought they were just not looking. I'll get an update soon."

Dolph was waiting for us on his porch, a scowl on his face like we'd kept him waiting hours. I didn't feel any emotions that matched the expression. He was putting on an act for the pack.

He ushered us into the kitchen and served coffee before asking if we'd solved the case.

"Where is Mark?" I asked, because I didn't want him barging in and finding out we'd basically gone over his head.

"On the other side of the island," Lance said. "Your tip about those two paths led him to the earth witch village."

Or he ended up there after entering one of the blanks. No matter, he was out of the way for long enough.

Lance started the conversation. "We'd like to talk to Stella and Kris. It will save time if you call them to us."

"You expect them to resist?" Dolph's annoyance at being ordered around by a rival was tightly tamped down. Unless Lance could scent emotions, he'd never know.

"We don't have time to deal with it if they do balk," I said. "There are a few more things."

"I'll tell them to meet you at The Howling Place. Is lunch today acceptable?"

We agreed. It gave us a few hours to do more investigating and for Destroyer to find anything he could about the blanks.

"What else?" he asked. "I do not have all day."

"We have some more information about the blackmail," Lance said. "It seems a witch touched the paper, and only a witch. Have you made enemies? Someone who would like to see you deposed?"

What was with these two? Lance could have chosen a dozen other ways to tell his alpha and he decided to so in the most confrontational way possible.

"I do not make enemies," Dolph said calmly.

He was feeling the exact opposite to calm. "I'm sure you don't," I said. "But it does look like a witch was angry enough to try to frame you."

He turned his gaze on me, and I swallowed to stop myself from squeaking. So this was the actual alpha energy.

I glared back; I would not let him intimidate me.

"Or afraid enough," he said. "How does this help you find Aria's killer?"

At least this time Lance kept quiet. I glanced over at Lilibeth and D. Both looked away like they could pretend they weren't there. Cowards.

"We don't know yet. Maybe nothing," I said. Time to tell him the last piece of information before the entire conversation became a fight about reputations. "I thought you wanted to know. There is one more item. You may have already noticed, or your trackers may have told you."

"What? Stop dancing around it." I guess once his alpha mojo was engaged, it was hard to turn it off.

"There are blank places on the island," I said. I added the details we had, and that Destroyer was investigating.

All aggression disappeared. "And you think Aria was killed in one of these spaces?"

"The path leads to one," Lance said. "They are not only blank of magic, or scents, but they transport you. We entered one not far from here and found ourselves near the medical clinic. Halfway across the island."

Dolph was silent. He looked out through the windows to the trees beyond his house. I didn't know what to do. His emotions shut down as soon as Lance finished talking.

After a few minutes, he turned back to us. "Who else knows?"

"Mrs. Vestum," I said. "A lot of animals. I don't know who might have figured it out. Anyone who went into the any of the spaces and ended up elsewhere."

"I would have heard. This is good. We need to keep this secret as long as we can."

"It's dangerous to do that," Lance said. He stood and his body shimmered, then settled.

30

"I am your alpha, and you will do as I say," Dolph shouted. His form shimmered too.

D took my elbow and pulled me to the side. "They are going to lose control and shift," he said.

"You are putting the entire pack in danger." Lance stepped around the counter to face Dolph. "The entire island. What happened to the vows made when we arrived?"

"I determine what actions we take," Dolph said, taking a step toward Lance. "If you wish to challenge my leadership, then you know what to do."

Both shifters shimmered. This time, I saw the wolves they would become if they lost full control.

Lance stepped back, but not like he was afraid. It was like he was making room.

"Stop it," I said into the boiling silence. "This is not going to help."

For a long moment, I thought they hadn't heard me. I shook off D's hand, determined to get between the shifters and stop this nonsense.

The shimmering stopped, and both turned to me as I approached.

"This does not concern you, witch," Dolph snarled at me.

"It's my home," I said. "You do not make decisions for the whole island. If you want us to find the murderer, you'll have to put your ego aside."

I held my breath. Dolph was the one I needed to bring back from the edge. Lance would follow if he calmed down. I'd talk to him later about what was going on.

Dolph blinked, and I caught a trace of the fire burning inside him. I sent a wish out to the universe that he wasn't too far gone.

He took a deep breath and turned to Lance. "She is right. We will speak later about your attitude."

It took Lance a few moments longer to get himself under control, but when he did, he apologized to me, not Dolph.

"I don't agree about it being kept a secret," I said. "We can't, anyway. These areas aren't isolated enough. And with a search for a killer going on, someone will stumble into one soon. Mrs. Vestum is searching for information or a cure."

"If you broadcast this news, many people will investigate out of curiosity," Dolph said. "What is your plan?"

I made one up on the spot and hoped the others would back me up. "Leave it with Mrs. V. I'll get something soon from Destroyer, and I'll pass it on to you as well."

Mrs. V joining the team had a benefit I hadn't anticipated. He didn't argue, just grunted and reached for his phone. We'd gained some credibility, or I guess she had that, and we just borrowed it.

Dolph typed out a text and put his phone to the side. "I will let you know if Mark has stumbled on one of these areas. I cannot guarantee he will be willing to keep the news secret as we wish, but I will try to persuade him."

The best we could ask for, no surprises. "As soon as I hear from Destroyer, I will tell you what his birds found."

"I find it a little disconcerting that the birds are organizing," Dolph said. "Let's hope no one has given the crows a reason to seek revenge."

I'd never thought of it that way. Yes, I'd done some research in my very tiny allotment of down time. Crows were intelligent. They recognized people. They brought gifts if they thought of you as a friend. They had funerals, and they committed murder.

"I'll try to keep a lid on any vengeance, but I don't think anyone should be worried. I get the feeling that the other birds are happy to fly around looking for clues but will draw the line at becoming hit men for the crows."

Dolph's phone pinged. "Stella and Kris will meet you at The Howling Place."

31

"What kind of relationship does Dolph have with Stella or Kris?" I asked as we walked to Sheena's bar. I tried not to think of them as a couple. They weren't, but the fact they'd both arrived back on Henbane around the same time was tying them together in my mind. It was our job to figure out how the affected the case.

"Stella is his aunt too," Lance said. "We're cousins. I forget you don't know things like that. Don't read too much into it, Cossi. He doesn't treat her like anything special. Shifter families are never really close."

Good to know. Although, knowing Lance and Dolph were cousins went a long way to explaining their relationship. "And Kris? I think we need to know as much as possible before we talk to them."

"They were friends once, right?" Lilibeth said. "I never knew what happened."

"Kris was friends with a lot of people," D said. "Phillip. Your parents, Cossi. A few of the earth witches. He was like a politician that way. No enemies, at least none I know about.

All kinds of friends, but I'd guess most were acquaintances, no more."

"How long has he been gone?" I asked. "Enough that he might be separate from everything that's going on? A fresh eye, maybe?"

"That's the weird part," Lance said. "Around the time your parents left. Don't think it's all connected, Cossi. Lots of things happened around that time. It's not like your mother made a mistake in a vacuum. People come and go. But he didn't run. He withdrew, I guess. Stayed with Dolph. We saw him here and there, and suddenly it was a year, and no one had seen him."

Could I believe him when he said not everything is tied to my mother's mistake, or to the murders, or to whoever is pulling the strings behind the scenes?

Sheena brought over a plate of appetizers and cider for everyone as soon as we sat. "You're expecting two more, I'll bring drinks when they get here."

"It would be better if they came separately," I said. "We have different questions for each of them, right?"

"How deep do you want to get?" D asked. "They just got back, so was it before Aria's murder, or are they suspects?"

"Is one of them being blackmailed?" I figured that was the trickiest question. "Maybe Sheena will let us use her office if we need to split them up."

Sheena arrived with two pints of ale and a bowl of nuts. "Your guests are almost here. I haven't seen Stella since she got back. Or Kris, come to think of it, but that's not a surprise."

Her prescience was working, because a few minutes later a tall, raven-haired man walked through the doors and looked around until he saw us. He strode over, took a seat and drank half the ale. "I needed that."

Before any of us could react, our second guest joined us. A woman with long, straight, dark red hair who bent to kiss Lance on the cheek before sitting. "Good to see you, nephew. Now why did Dolph demand we meet?"

I was glad they'd warned me about how shifters didn't act like what I thought was normal family members. I'd hoped Lance would start the questioning, but he smiled back at me and nodded. When did I become the spokeswitch?

"You know about Aria?" I asked. Not actually stalling but getting us on the same page, so to speak.

"Since when did Henbane become a place where people get murdered?" Kris asked. "And why isn't Mark here? He's the police, right?"

"Relax, Kris," Stella said. "If the alpha wants us to talk to these kids, then we do. Ask your questions. I'm sure Kris also has other things to do."

What to start with? Do you have an alibi? Are you being blackmailed? Did you create the blank spaces? I guess the third question was off the list because we'd promised not to spread rumors. And if anything changed later, we could still ask.

"I guess we should start with why you came back?" I asked. "You've both been away for a long time."

"I finished my job," Kris said. "I left to complete a mission for the alpha. I will not tell you what that entailed. I arrived back three days ago. Aria was dead already."

I watched as D entered everything in the database. We could check the facts easily.

"And you?" I prompted Stella.

"I missed my family," she said, reaching out to touch Lance's arm.

He pulled away. "Don't lie, Stella. You came back for a reason. Family isn't that much of a draw."

"Bitter," she said to him. "He's right, though. I came back because I needed a home. I've been wandering for a while. Visiting other communities, looking for purpose. I was left with nowhere else to go."

"When did you get here?" Lilibeth asked.

"I met Kris on the mainland. We arrived together. Dear Aria was gone. And everyone was searching for a clue."

"Where are you staying?" I asked. If she was looking for a home, did that mean she had one here?

"Dolph gave me a cottage close by his home," Stella said.

"I've been in my cabin," Kris said. "I'm a solitary. The only shifter one, as a matter of fact."

Stella had more access to Dolph's home, and his compost heap, but she wasn't a witch. Kris had more access to witches, but he was outside the village.

I pulled up the picture of the note. "Do either of you know anything about this?"

Stella leaned in, then shook her head. "Something juicy, but not me, dear."

Kris glared at me. "Where did you find this?"

32

"An animal found it," I said. I wasn't about to give him any details about my sources. "My power allows me to speak all languages, including animals."

"Stella, you can go," Kris said. "It appears I'm the one they are seeking."

"I would love to stay," she said. "Perhaps I can help?"

"I will not be the subject of gossip," he said. "If you will not leave, we will go somewhere more private."

I was okay with her going because we could find her later if we needed to. The most important thing right now was Kris's confession. He was furious but managed to keep it off his face.

"I'm sure Sheena would let us use her office," I said.

Stella stood and straightened her blouse to cover her disappointment. "Fine. Good luck with your investigation."

When the door closed behind her, Kris ran his fingers through his hair. "I am not proud of this," he said.

"Let's start with who is blackmailing you," I said. "If it's too public here, we can go to Lance's place. It's only a short walk away."

He looked around, and a wave of relief hit me. "It's fine. I assume you will have to tell Dolph, and Mark."

"Dolph for sure," Lance said. "It's pack business if you are being forced to pay or do something. Mark? If it has nothing to do with the murder, then he doesn't need to know."

"I was a wild pup," Kris said. "I have no idea who gave me the note. I have no idea which indiscretion they refer to, but there are many. I can assure you that I did not kill Aria."

"We need Mark," D said.

"You said you would not," Kris said.

"His power," D said, holding up his hands. "I meant that he could tell who was lying to us."

Kris looked like he was going to argue. His feelings didn't change, so it was just an act. I didn't mention what I read to anyone. My reading of his emotions wasn't as reliable as Mark's power to see lies, but I didn't get the vibe that he was lying. Well, about anything important to the case. He believed that the blackmail had nothing to do with Aria's murder, but I'd put money on the fact he knew exactly what and who.

"It's fine," I said. "We know where to find you if we need something more."

"I do not answer to witches or Lance," Kris said.

"You do answer to Dolph," Lilibeth said, "and he is expecting results."

He scanned the room as if expecting Dolph to march in and reprimand him. No one was paying attention to us. No one entered the bar.

"If my Alpha needs me, of course I will answer." He pushed away from the table.

"I suggest you tell him what you know about the black-mail," D said. So I wasn't the only one who thought Kris lied about it.

"I suppose it will be better coming from me," Kris said. "I will go now."

He walked out without another word.

"We forgot to ask them about the blank spaces," Lance said. "Those appeared after both of them returned home."

How would we keep them from spreading the news?

"We can ask later," I said. "I should be hearing from Destroyer soon. In fact, he should have reported already. Give me a second."

What if the search had somehow banished all the birds from the island? Or trapped them inside? Or, broken my link with my familiar?

33

"Destroyer." I said the word aloud so they knew what was going on rather than just stare at me.

"I'm on the way. Come outside."

I checked with Sheena if my crow could come inside, and she told me all familiars were welcome as long as they behaved.

He was already on the ground when I opened the door. I invited him inside and promised a little beer to refresh him.

He waddled across the floor to our table. Lance already had a bowl of beer on the floor.

"Tell me what you found, first," I said.

"We found the place the shifter was killed, I think," he said. "You can't go there."

I translated to the others. "Why can't we go in there?"

"In one of the places you asked us to search." He took a couple of steps closer to the bowl. "We will confirm and find a way to bring you or Roy's witch to it."

"Animals aren't affected?" D asked as I passed on the information.

"Birds and four-footed creatures are not. Maybe you are not strong enough to overcome the spell."

D pulled out his phone and started typing. "I'm sending this to Mrs. V. If it's a spell, she needs details to find a counter."

"Tell me everything you know about the areas," I said. "We have someone working on trying to fix them."

"That's good idea. If only murderers and animals can go in, then more people will die." Destroyer dipped his beak in the beer.

I listened to his description and translated as he talked.

"A squirrel said it smelled like someone burned sage all over the ground. Like when witches clear bad energies from places. The trees and ground look normal, but some spots are too dry and others are too wet. The balance is not healthy. Maybe the magic of the spell is upsetting things."

"Any sounds or other scents?" Lance asked.

"We did not hear unusual sounds, no other animals reported smells. There are new stones." He sipped more beer.

"We should go to Mrs. V," I said. "She'll know what to ask."

D looked up from his phone. "She just texted that," he said, pointing to the text on his screen. "But she also wants to know about the stones."

"Can't bring them to you, too heavy," Destroyer said. "And you probably can't go to them because of the spell."

"What do they look like?" D asked.

"White, but maybe not because we don't see in colors. Light color, not painted, but naturally. Nothing special but that." Destroyer peered into the now empty bowl. "Perhaps I can remember more if there is more beer."

I laughed. "Tell us everything and you can drink more before we go to Mrs. Vestum's to answer more questions."

"Stones are on the edge of the places you cannot go. We watched a witch come near, and before they got to the stone, they turned around and walked away. That is all."

Lance brought another half bowl of Destroyer's favorite beer. D sent the last bit of information to Mrs. V and let her know we were on our way.

"There might be a way," Lilibeth said. She'd been listening to us without commenting the entire time. "What if an animal led one of us in? Or a shifter in wolf form? With our eyes closed. Cossi, don't let Destroyer drink so much."

Sounds like one of us meant me since none of the others spoke animal.

34

I let Destroyer ride my shoulder after pulling on a jacket to protect my skin. He said he was fine to fly, but I didn't trust him because he was leaning against the chair leg as he said it. No drunken flying on my watch.

Mrs. V opened the door as I was parking my bike outside her place. Beulah was getting a workout today because after this, I was going to try for one of those weird rocks. No matter what else happened.

"Come in and don't argue until I've explained."

I tried to balk but she grabbed my arm and pulled me through the door, shutting it behind me.

"Your familiar is drunk," she said.

"Yes. What do you need to explain?" She wasn't going to get away with stalling after locking me in.

"I can fix that; you need him fully operating for this." She marched into the kitchen, not once turning back to see if I followed.

Of course I did. She'd never been on the defensive with me before — mostly it was the opposite.

Mark sat at the table. No Roy, but his notebook was open on the table. They'd been discussing the case.

"Tell the bird to drink this and then wait outside," Mrs. V said as she placed a saucer of water on the floor.

It carried the scent of a stream that ran through ferns and moss. I told Destroyer and lifted him from my shoulder. He hopped to the saucer and sucked it all up.

"Outside now!" Mrs. V opened the back door. Destroyer flew through and she closed it. "He'll be fine once the tea works."

Enough delay. We had things to talk about when Mark left, and he was leaving. "Why is he here?" I didn't care how it sounded or if he was hurt. Yes, we'd dated, but this was more important.

"I decided it's time for you to work together," she said. "After the news this afternoon, you need the authorities on your side."

He didn't say anything. How was I supposed to remind her we didn't trust him? "You should have told me, not sprung it on me. I don't like those kinds of surprises."

"There was no time, girl. We need to see the murder site, and he is the island police. I've told him what we know."

She bustled around the kitchen while she spoke. She was nervous, and I found it scarier than her usual attitude. If the person who was protecting the paranormal world was afraid, I should just do as she says, right?

"And has he given us any information?" I asked. "No, thanks. I don't want tea."

"Cossi, sit down," Mark said. "Mrs. Vestum, you too."

I figured this would be over faster if I stopped resisting. "Do you have anything to contribute to the investigation?" I asked him.

"Is there anything you don't know?" he asked. "You went to Dolph behind my back."

Was Dolph in on this? I didn't think so. This was all Mrs. V. "He summoned us. And I don't know what I don't know."

"The cause of death?" he asked. Mark was doing his best to keep from telling us anything we didn't already know.

"Beaten to death. Maybe poisoned or under a weakening spell," I said.

"I'm stumped," Mark said. "You know everything if Mrs. V is up to date. You found out more than I did, even sneaking around."

He was holding something back. That wasn't a guess on my part. I read it like a black spot in his emotions. I hadn't seen emotions as colors before, but now his frustration was blazing orange, this secret was a black blotch, and he didn't want to keep it either. Mrs. V's fear was a trembling lavender. Just what I needed, a new development in my powers when I had no time to explore them.

"So you know about the blank areas? And that a shifter is being blackmailed?"

"I didn't tell him who," Mrs. Vestum said, "but he knew Stella and Kris were back. They've been eliminated as suspects."

Mark's phone rang. He looked at the screen and sent it to voicemail.

"Cossi, I need to be there when you go to where Aria was killed," he said. "My job is to find the killer."

His phone rang again, and he sent it to voicemail again before turning the ringer off. He rubbed his temples as he put the phone away, as if he'd developed a headache trying to convince me.

"We're going there now," I said. "You can come, but you'll wait until I've experimented. If we can't break whatever spell is on the place, we can't get in without help. And there are only so many of them who are big enough to assist, anyway."

"Agreed," he said. "I'll get Roy to meet us there. He'll be the best bet to lead you. If it can be done at all."

I went to the back door and opened it for a very sorry Destroyer to hop in.

"Where are we going?" I asked him so we could tell Roy.

"I've already told the dog to meet us," he said before turning a beady eye on Mrs. Vestum. "You are forgiven, witch."

She thanked him and told me to wait. She left Mark and me in the kitchen together. We didn't talk. He was capable of separating personal from professional life, but I wasn't. I'd need a cooling off period before our next date.

"Don't touch the stone," Mrs. Vestum said as she rejoined us with a bundle of cloth in her hands. "We have no idea what it will do to you. Use these gloves and place it in this bag after someone takes pictures and sends them to me."

R oy was waiting for us at the entrance to the closest blank space. It looked like just another part of the forest to me. Destroyer told me to stand still until he showed Roy the location of a stone. "I don't want you wandering off by mistake."

Mark stood with me and watched as the two animals slipped between the trees, Destroyer riding on Roy's back.

"When we have it," he said, "I'll take the pictures. It's more official that way. And I have an evidence bag."

I guess it made sense to keep things under his authority, unless he decided once again to cut me out. Making things official meant there would be less to argue when the killer came to justice. "And where will you send it for analysis?"

He grinned at me. "The same place I would normally," he said.

I knew he was baiting me, but I couldn't help reacting. "What about working together?"

He laughed at me. "Mrs. Vestum is where I take evidence for analysis."

I didn't care that he was making fun of me as long as we

didn't lose the chance to remove the spell. And I didn't argue because I wasn't exactly excited about going in now that we were here.

Just as Roy and Destroyer returned, Lance, D, and Lilibeth rode up. "If you don't come back fast, we'll go looking for you," D said. "Tell Destroyer we'll follow him to find you."

Having my friends with me gave me confidence. I passed on the instructions to my familiar.

"I understood them," he said. "It won't work. Shifter should go. In dog."

"You can speak human?" That was new, and probably a good thing.

"Learning. I told you crows were the most intelligent bird."

"You can talk to him directly," I said to the others.

Roy sat and waited for instruction. "He needs to tell me I am allowed to do this," he said.

"Mark, he's waiting for permission," I said, assuming the 'he' Roy meant was his partner.

"This is part of the investigation," Mark said. "Do as she asks until I tell you otherwise."

Roy walked over and nudged my hand. "Ready?"

I ignored the qualifier Mark used. He'd included me and pushed me away too many times for me to expect anything else.

"I have to keep my eyes closed," I said.

Mark handed me a blindfold. "It's too easy for you to open them if you stumble. Use this. Roy will make sure you're safe."

I really didn't want to wear the black cloth. It felt too much like someone was controlling me. I didn't want to wander into another part of the island either, so I handed the cloth to D. "You can tie it on," I said.

When I was essentially cut off from seeing the world, I hesitated long enough to try to bring up scents and sounds. It made the whole experiment a little more comfortable when I caught the scent of dog, and pine. I reached out my hand for Roy to guide me.

"Wait," Mark said. "The gloves."

"In my backpack," I said. "I can't reach it."

Someone pulled the straps off my shoulder and then placed a glove in my right hand. "Put them on," Lance said. "We'll keep your pack here. That way you'll be less likely to get unbalanced."

Good idea, I thought as I pulled the gloves on one at a time, awkwardly, because I couldn't see. If I fell, I'd probably pull off the blindfold without thinking.

"One more thing," Mark said.

My other senses were picking up more the longer I couldn't see. I recognized Mark's emotions before he spoke.

He pressed the blindfold closer to the bridge of my nose and then whispered two words. "It won't come off now. Until I release it."

"What?" Adrenalin flooded my veins. "No. Release it now. You didn't tell me you were going to do that."

He placed his hands on my shoulders. "Cossi, you are right. I didn't tell you because of exactly what's happening now. I will remove it as soon as you are safely back. I don't want to take the chance you'll see anything in there that sends you away. We don't know if it's a trap. You didn't even think of that, right?"

"No, we didn't," Lance said. "A trap for Cossi? Why?"

"She's the one who's been finding the murderers," Mark said. "If you were Aria's killer, wouldn't you want her gone?"

My whole body was shaking with the effect of all the adrenalin and nowhere to put it. "Should I even go in?"

"Keep Destroyer on your shoulder," Mark said.

"Don't let go of Roy," Lilibeth said. "Be quick and just retrieve a rock. No going exploring."

Mark's hands squeezed my shoulders. "I think it will be okay if you don't touch the stone with your skin. Be careful and stay with the animals. If something goes wrong, we know they can get out. We can still follow them, even without talking to them."

I took a deep breath and shook out my limbs. It didn't calm me much, but I guess a little paranoia was an asset. "Okay, let's do this."

36

I touched Roy's head.

"Grab my collar," he said. "We will take care of you."

Destroyer warned me before landing on my shoulder. I took a firm grip and tried to remember the ground between me and the entrance to the path. Flat, mostly dirt and grass. The animals had only been gone for a few minutes.

I would be fine.

I will be fine.

I am fine.

The affirmations were wasted breath; I didn't believe them and was pretty sure everything was about to go sideways.

We went slowly. Destroyer gave me clear instructions on how to navigate the roots that would have landed me on my ass. After what felt like hours, though probably less than five minutes, Roy came to a stop.

"Kneel," he said. "One of the rocks is in front of your left hand. You can let go of me. I will not move."

If this was a trap, now was the most likely time for it to

spring. I knelt, and dampness soaked my jeans. This must be one of the wetter than usual places I'd been told about.

"Reach for it," Destroyer said. "A little to your right. Now reach down. That's it."

It was a stone about the size of a bagel, but not round. No jagged edges. Not heavy for me.

"Am I still with you?" I asked. The forest sounded and smelled the same, but I could be in another place. I mean, how different could one group of trees be from another?

"Yes. No trap, I suppose," Destroyer said. "Stand. Reach for the dog and we will turn you around."

Going back seemed much faster. Probably because I wasn't worried that I'd fall down a pit.

As soon as Roy said I was safe, I called Mark over. "Get this thing off me."

He put his hand on my left shoulder, avoiding the hand holding the rock, and pressed the blindfold again. It released and he slipped it over my head.

I looked at what I held in my gloved hands. It was a rock, orange, not white. Shaped a bit like a lozenge, but more natural. I carefully turned it over and heard a gasp from everyone.

"Hang on," Mark said. He held up his phone and took a picture. "Turn it over."

He sent the ten or so pictures to Mrs. V before holding out the bag she'd provided and then dropped the whole thing in the plastic evidence container.

"Why did you all react like that?" I said as I dropped it inside. There was a sigil on the bottom painted in black that I didn't understand. Just a single mark in what seemed to be black nail polish.

"It means death," D said. "If all the rocks have sigils, they could be the actual spell."

I wasn't going back inside that space even one more step without a very strong reason. Let alone the other places. Yes, finding the spell was a good reason, but we could surely find another way.

Mark's phone pinged.

"Mrs. Vestum needs the rock now. And says don't go back in."

"I'm good with that," I said. "It's possible we can get animals to gather them and drag them to where we can pick them up easily."

37

Mrs. Vestum had a plate of cookies and freshly brewed coffee waiting for us. I'd managed to ride to her place without passing out from adrenalin withdrawal, but only that. I was shaking again when we arrived.

Mark handed her the evidence bag and then poured me coffee. "Sit and have some cookies."

Mrs. V stared at the stone inside the plastic bag. "We will need them all," she said. "Did you ask about animals retrieving them?"

"Destroyer will experiment," I said. "We don't want to make it worse by extending the spaces. He'll have a raccoon bring one from the same area to where we were standing. They won't be able to tell if it makes a difference, but Lance stayed behind for that purpose."

"Good. Let me know if they are successful. And Lance can send pictures of the sigils on each stone." She looked at me. "Where are the gloves?"

"I left them with him. I figured he shouldn't touch them either."

"Did anything happen to them?"

I hadn't noticed any change, but I wasn't really paying attention. "No? What were you expecting?"

"That there would be a reaction," she said. "But Lance will notice, I'm sure."

"So what do we do next?" D asked.

"Wait to hear from Lance," I said. "But we have to clear these stones, right? Before the spell does real damage?"

She nodded. "Eat more of the cookies. I will place this somewhere safe until we need it again."

Mark's phone started vibrating. He looked at the screen and swore. Then he put it in airplane mode.

"Who's trying to reach you?" I asked.

"No one more important than solving these cases," he said.

I would have asked more but Destroyer interrupted my thoughts.

"It worked. The pictures are coming. We arranged for the stone to come to you."

Mrs. V came back into the room just as I passed on his report. "Excellent. I have an idea how we do this. Tell Lance to shift and try to retrieve a stone as a wolf."

I did, and we waited.

"Will you be able to tell who cast the spell?" I asked.

"It will take some time," she said. "If my idea works, not as long as it would if we have to send you to retrieve them. Your inexperience with our ways excuses you, Cossi, but I question why none of your companions were able to come up with the solution I have."

The others shrank away from her judgment. Even though she didn't blame me, I felt lacking. I knew she'd tell us soon enough, so I grabbed another cookie, chocolate chip with hazelnuts, and stuffed my mouth as an excuse not to speak.

"It worked," Destroyer said. "He has contacted the Alpha to arrange shifters to collect the stones."

I passed it on, and tried not to show Mrs. V that I should have thought of it no matter that I was new to the island. Of course the shifters would be able to do this.

"Does that mean a shifter must have placed them?" I asked, feeling pretty good that I'd thought of it at least.

"The odds are high," she said, "but a witch could have built protections against being a victim of their own spell."

"Destroyer," I said aloud this time, "can the birds search all the affected places to see if someone is nearby?"

"The murderer? Yes, once again the bird army will save the day."

I told them he would, leaving out the part about him taking the credit. "We've removed two of the sigils; that must have set off an alarm, right?"

"See, when you pay attention, you are capable of rational thought," Mrs. V said.

No one else spoke, but D winked at me. If she was going to be part of the team, Mrs. V really needed to tone down the meanness. I was not going to tell her that; I wanted to live a long and healthy life.

"It might not be the killer," I said, including Destroyer in the comment. "Let's not get our hopes up. By now, anyone could have discovered something was wrong and tried to investigate."

"Shifter in one of the far spots," Destroyer said. "In dog form. Sniffing at rocks."

I passed the report on. "Any idea who?" I asked.

"The eagle who found the shifter does not know the

name. I have taught them it is important to observe their world. Stranger."

"Can the eagle describe him?" I crossed my fingers, hoping that it meant something in the magical world.

"Silver fur, something wrong with front leg. Smells like female. Larger than your pet dogman."

I was very glad Lance couldn't understand Destroyer.

I asked if anyone knew the shifter. Mark had his phone in his hand again. It vibrated but he was typing a text. "Dolph doesn't recognize them. He would know if she was a member of his pack."

We gathered our things. "Keep an eye on her," I told Destroyer. "We're on our way."

"At the one near the earth witch village. I will meet you at the entrance and guide you from there. The shifters have arrived here. They brought boxes for the stones. Lance will tell them what to do."

"Mrs. Vestum needs the rocks," I said. He wouldn't be able to pass that on, but a quick text to Lance took care of it.

"She might not be the killer," Mark said as we rode. Lilibeth and D were behind us. No one wanted to be left out.

"Dolph doesn't know they're here," I said. "A shifter the alpha doesn't know is suddenly on the island. That can't be anything but bad news."

"But it doesn't mean she's the killer," he insisted.

It would be the mother of all coincidences if she wasn't, but I didn't have the breath to argue.

"How are we going to find her?" I asked. "All she has to do is stay inside the border of the spell. There aren't enough of us to guard the entire perimeter."

"Wait until we get there," he said.

It didn't take more than ten minutes before Destroyer told me where to stop. "On your feet," he said. "Wheels won't work."

When we met him at the edge of the forest, I could see one of the stones only ten feet away. I didn't feel like wandering off, so we should be safe. I held up my hand to stop Mark from moving closer to it.

"We need you with us," I said. "Okay, Destroyer, what's the plan?"

"We have cleared one area, and the spell is gone there. The shifter told me his plan, but I don't know if it is good. I am not built to speak human."

"I'll translate when you tell me." I hated waiting on anything when we were this close to catching the killer, but he knew more about the spell than any of us.

"I will observe her," he said. "An eagle is watching now, but they cannot talk to anyone who is far. We will leave the spell in place here. Shifters will go in and take her. You will know what to do from there."

I told D, Lilibeth, and Mark what Lance came up with. "I don't like it," I said. "We're on the outside. She's strong enough to have already killed one shifter."

"And we're not sure they'll bring her out alive," Mark said.

"Or who will be there," Lilibeth said. "Dolph won't sit it out easily."

"You are too fragile to go in," Destroyer said. "I will not allow it."

What the heck? He never tried to order me around. "How are you going to stop me?"

"What did he say?" Lilibeth asked.

I told her.

"Oh. Yeah, you wouldn't know. If you get hurt, he will too. Not like physically, but just pain."

"I will be careful," I said to my familiar. "We can't let this go wrong."

A red wolf ran through the undergrowth and skidded to a stop. He shifted into Lance. An eagle dropped a bundle of clothes and flew away.

"New plan," Lance said as he pulled on the pants.

"Dolph is in charge of clearing the other sites. He didn't like it, but we reached a compromise."

"Dolph compromising? How did he get the eagle to bring your clothes?" I didn't mean to sidetrack, but if others could communicate with the birds it would help. I ignored the little bump of jealousy.

"I told the crows to listen to the shifters and witches. Gossip is entertaining." Destroyer seemed to have lost his panic about me getting hurt.

"A crow was flapping around," Lance said. "Going from one of the pack who'd shifted to me. I guessed. When I stripped down, an eagle landed. Dolph rolled my clothes so the eagle could carry them."

Destroyer wasn't the only smart bird on Henbane. I did not pass on that thought. At least I hoped he didn't read my mind.

"What's the plan?" Mark asked.

"Some of the pack will be here any second. We'll remove stones so you have a path. We tested it, and moving them breaks the confusion. We'll capture her, you watch. We'll take her to Mark's and then question her."

"And Dolph is okay with that?" Mark asked.

"His plan," Lance said. "He'll be there for questioning, but she's not his pack as far as he can tell."

"And if she turns out to be a lost one?" I asked. "What then?"

"Look," Lance said, "his alpha power will have some effect on any shifter, so he'll be useful. If she's a lost pack member? He's bound by the oaths."

"Destroyer, will this new plan work for you?" I wasn't going to let him get hurt. If he needed me to stay here, I would. I'm not saying I'd be happy, but at least there would be witches to make sure no shifter went too far.

"Stay out of the action. We'll be fine. Just remember, you can be picked up and dropped to the side by an eagle, or even a big owl."

Three other shifters arrived in human form. Lance joined them. "We'll come back when the path is clear. Be ready to move fast."

Then there were four piles of clothes on the ground and four wolves running to the trees.

Lilibeth and I stuffed the clothes into our backpacks and waited.

A wolf slunk back into the light. Not Lance, but he looked directly at me and said, "Come."

We followed him through the trees, turning to the right just inside. Snarls and the sounds of branches breaking reached me before I saw the action. Our guide ran to join the fight as a black shadow swooped down to land on my backpack, almost tipping me over.

"It won't take long," Destroyer said. "They are trying to weaken her, so she'll shift to human, but it's not working."

"How else will they be able to capture her?"

Four wolves attacking one, and they weren't winning?

"They'll hurt her," he said, "unless you have an idea."

I passed the question on. "Someone will be badly hurt if this goes on," I said.

Mark reached into his pack and pulled out a small gun. Then he loaded a dart. "Tell them to move away," he said.

"Lance, move," I yelled, hoping the others would follow him.

Suddenly the strange shifter was snapping at air. The four wolves had withdrawn to growl and bare their teeth from a distance.

I heard kind of a wheeze, then another. Two feathery objects bloomed in her side. She bit at them, but her energy was already draining. Two steps later, she stumbled, shimmered, and then a woman lay on the ground. Long blond hair tangled around her like a dress.

We got the shifter to Mark's place and in the single cell. I hadn't thought about it when I first came because it was behind a door. I'd assumed his bedroom and bathroom were there. This official area was in a wide corridor with a door at the end. I wasn't going exploring, so that could lead to Narnia as far as I was concerned.

Doctor Rene checked her out and pronounced her healthy enough to withstand an interrogation, but not for long periods.

Mark led the questioning with Dolph at his side. Mrs. V and I stood behind them. We were under orders to keep quiet, but I shared a look with Mrs. Vestum that I hoped she understood that we would do what we liked.

"Your name?" Mark asked.

"I'm not on a list somewhere?"

Despite the silver wolf she shifted into, the killer was probably a bit younger than me. I felt all the rage and confusion of a teenager, but I'd guess she was in her early twenties. Since it's so hard to tell the age of a magical person, that was the best I could do.

To have committed murder so young meant she'd live a couple of centuries in the secret prison.

"There is no list," Dolph said. "Answer his questions."

"Carly Devers," she said. "Why did I answer that?"

"I am an alpha," Dolph said. "I can compel you. Don't waste our time."

"Carly," Mark asked again, "did you set the spell stones?"

"Yes."

Apparently, the compulsion didn't cover expanding on the answer.

"Why?" Mark asked.

This might be important, but we'd already guessed she was the culprit. Why didn't he ask about the murder?

"To draw a witch to me."

"Why?"

Maybe he'd wear her down with these questions so the important ones would be easier? Dolph should just order her to give full answers.

"To get revenge," Carly said. She turned away and I got a wave of frustration from her.

"Answer in full," Dolph said. "You are not helping yourself by fighting."

The frustration turned to acceptance.

"My mother was forced to flee Henbane. She was pregnant with me. My father doesn't know I exist. We have no pack to join. She decided it was safer to pass as human." The words came out as though escaping her grasp. "She died. I found out we were suppressing our shifter nature with a potion. It stopped coming."

"Who was providing it?" Dolph asked.

"Leanne Macy."

And she was the first victim.

"Was she the witch you wanted to trap?" Mark asked.

Carly gripped the bars and pulled herself close. "Not her. She was helping, then I found out she was murdered. The one who is behind everything. The one who forced my mother off the island and out of the pack."

"Who was your mother?" Dolph asked. "You are part of my pack no matter what happened."

"The last name doesn't ring a bell?" She screamed the words

I guess there were ways around just answering questions.

"If you don't know the right name, then you are lying. I suppose my power over you is not absolute." Dolph took a step forward.

"Leah." The name came out through clenched teeth.

"I am sorry to hear of her death," Dolph said. "Whoever forced her to leave is a powerful witch. Your father? Perhaps he is still here?"

She fought against his power.

It filled the small space like honey. I almost confessed every sin I even imagined committing. What must that be like as a shifter?

"Kris," she said. "Tamaska. He doesn't know."

"We will call him," Dolph said. "Rest for now. We are not finished with our questioning."

I wasn't going to just walk away. Why was he giving her time to recover? I stepped forward. Mrs. Vestum grabbed my hand. "No. We wait for her father."

40

D olph sent a text as we returned to the main part
of Mark's house. "He will arrive within a half
hour. I have not told him he has a daughter."

I gave D, Lilibeth, and Lance the update.

"Cossi," Mrs. Vestum said, "please join me outside. We
must talk."

She didn't sound mad, which was unusual. Just disap-
pointed.

I grabbed two glasses of water and joined her on the
porch.

"Thank you," she said. "I need to ask you about your
training. In there, you displayed a complete lack of knowledge of shifter behavior. What has Phillip taught you about
alphas?"

I didn't want to rat him out. The fact he'd laid off with
the heavy training allowed me to do all kinds of things I
wanted. Like solving crimes. But she wasn't the first person
to question his methods. If everyone thought he was failing,
then maybe he was.

"I didn't mean to disrespect Dolph," I said.

"He did not take offense," she said. "If he had, you would know. Answer my question. You are not in trouble."

It was hard to believe her given our history. She'd sniped at me for almost three weeks, and now she was being all kind and interested. Yes, we'd agreed to find out who was behind all the killings, but I guess I hadn't really accepted she was an ally. It didn't matter because she was right, I needed to up my knowledge. Regardless of what was going on, I couldn't spend much more time in ignorance. For one thing, The Inner Spell would never succeed if I didn't know how things worked.

"He's been showing me how to run a business," I said. "I guess history and culture haven't been high on his list."

"They should be number one," she said. "Has he given you books?"

Kids books. And unreadable lists of spells and lineage. I told her the titles I remembered.

"You will never learn that way," she said. "I will speak to him when we've got this settled."

I remembered she'd threatened to replace him a day or two ago.

"I'm not sure that's a good idea," I said. "He's busy. And he was a friend to my parents." And I lived with him. If he got offended, would he kick me out?

"I am sure," she said. "Now here's our missing father. We should return to the interrogation."

41

"Where did she take you?" Kris asked.

We'd walked in expecting an interroga- tion, but Mark and Dolph were standing to the side. Kris stood at the bars, one hand through, holding Carly's fingers.

"We have given them a few minutes to reunite," Dolph said. "I am not sure if it is a kindness or a punishment. She will be in prison soon."

"If I had known, I would have found you," Kris said to his daughter. "Please tell me about your life."

"Why didn't mom tell you?" Carly asked. "Why didn't she tell me about you?"

Kris squeezed her hand and looked down. The emotions pouring off him were so muddled I couldn't interpret them.

"We'd been fighting," he said. "She was acting weirdly, and I demanded she tell me why, or what I'd done. Now, of course, I know. She was carrying my child. I don't know why she kept it secret, but she had no reason to run from me."

Carly pulled her fingers free and moved to the back of the cell.

"I grew up thinking she left because of you." A shudder of regret stopped her words for a moment. "I though you knew about me and made her leave."

"Never," Kris said. "I would have loved you."

"I've learned a lot since she died. How much she kept from me. Why we left and couldn't go back. Or be found. It wasn't you. It was a witch."

"You are back now," Kris said. He turned to Mark and Dolph. "Can we find a way to keep her here on Henbane?"

"The murder is not the only crime," Dolph said. "She didn't contact the pack when she came home. She set magical traps that disturbed the health of our island. And you know that I have no authority on this. We are bound by the rules of the island. The council will make the decision. I will ensure you are there to make your plea."

It was all said kindly. Dolph didn't want this damaged child to be punished. His annoyingly arrogant energy was tightly controlled.

"There are many reasons for the council to be merciful, Kris," Mark said. "We need her to tell us everything, and I will ask for leniency."

"If she goes to prison, I will go with her," Kris said. "She does not have to live her life so alone, no matter what the future holds."

Dolph ushered Kris back to join us. "Let Mark do his job," he said. "Her future is in her own hands now."

He rejoined Mark, and they commenced the interrogation again.

"Tell us what you know," Mark said. "I won't interrupt with questions until you finish."

Carly sat on the cot in the back. Her head down, letting her long hair fall like a curtain to hide her face. She clasped her hands in her lap and just breathed for a few minutes.

All her emotions drew into her core, and I couldn't read her any more than the others. So this was how people blocked me. Not a spell, just discipline.

"My mother didn't tell me anything until she was dying. We left Henbane because she'd seen something. An experiment went wrong, not by accident, but because someone sabotaged it. The person who did that was powerful and told the others what to do. Some stayed, some fled. Those who stayed agreed to a suppression spell. Mom said she thought they were compelled to agree."

I wanted to ask if my parents were there, but I knew they were. No one spoke of another disaster at the same time as my mother's mistake. I still thought of it that way even though Carly just said it wasn't only moments before.

"When she died, I found a letter." Carly wiped at her eyes, still hidden beneath her hair. "She explained everything. I didn't even know I was a shifter. Someone had been sending potions to stop the shifting. Leanne Macy. Mom said to keep taking them so I wouldn't shift. She told me where to find other shifters to train me and said I should stay away from here."

My heart squeezed. It was my story, except for the shifter thing.

"Then the potions didn't come," Carly said. "I called the number mom gave me and learned she'd been murdered."

The room was silent as she unfolded her story. I held my breath. She was going to tell us who was behind all of this. I would finally solve my biggest mystery: why my parents were forced to leave and why my third power was suppressed.

She took another deep breath. This one was a little jagged, as if it hurt.

"There were fifteen people involved in the event," Carly said. "Mom wrote the names down before they started. She said it was the smartest thing she ever did. Since leaving, she was unable to recreate it. Losing the original was her biggest fear."

After a long silence that had me fighting my urge to demand answers, Mark asked, "So you came here to capture the ringleader?"

Carly nodded. "Aria was on the list. I wanted her to tell me who sabotaged the experiment, but she couldn't. She was under the suppression spell. I couldn't control myself. I don't remember hitting her, but the next thing I knew, she was dead."

So, not a separate spell to weaken her. This was the same as the others who tried to tell us.

"Then you set the spells?"

"No. I was trying to figure out what to do. I heard some talking, not that close, but they would hear me if I made noise. I shifted and howled, and then ran."

"You didn't want her to be left without a burial?" Dolph asked.

"No. Nothing that happened to me was her fault. She was a victim, too. I will never forgive myself or whoever started this."

Long moments of silence again as everyone tried to absorb the news.

D squeezed my arm. "We'll figure this out," he whispered.

I leaned into him for comfort. All that was left was the list of names. Fifteen that night, six already dead.

"Who was on the list?" Mark asked.

Carly raised her eyes from the ground. Her face was

stained with tears. "Mr. and Mrs. Fortuna, Leanne Macy, Zeb Whitecliff," she murmured. "Mom's wasn't, but she was there."

"That leaves ten people," Mark said.

Carly nodded and opened her mouth to add names. Her eyes rolled back and she collapsed.

42

We were all sent out after Carly died. Mark told us to keep everything we learned under wraps because the knowledge was a reason for the killer to come after everyone in the room.

Kris stayed with her, waiting for Doctor Rene to check for cause of death. The case was solved, but another person was dead.

"We know there are ten names," D said. "Not the entire island. And it is a witch. She died trying to fix her mistake."

As far as I was concerned, we still needed to look at the entire island because we had no idea who any of them were. "I guess nine potential victims and one serial killer," I said.

"You could look at it that way," Lilibeth said. "I'm choosing to think of it as a step forward because Carly was trying."

I needed time alone to absorb the information. There was a powerful person on the island who had a secret to kill for. If we got too close, it wouldn't be nine possible murders; it would be us and anyone we might have told. By us, I included Mark, Dolph and Mrs. Vestum.

"I'm going home," I said. "I'm exhausted. See you later? Jan's for dinner?"

They agreed and we all split up. I thought at Destroyer as I walked.

"What?" he snapped. "The bad areas are all clear. The dog men have gone home. You caught the killer, and we all celebrate."

"Did you hear what happened in the cell?"

"Heard her words," he said. "We need rest if we are going to catch this person."

"We do. If I write this down, will you be able to hide it?"

"Bad idea."

"You can't talk to anyone else, but if something happens to me, you can give this to another witch, right?"

"Do not write it down. I will remember. If you die, I will not be able to give someone a note."

I was too tired to guess at his meaning. "Why not? I don't know much about our arrangement, remember? It would be nice if someone told me the things I need to know."

"I die," he said. "Familiar dies with witch."

"That sucks," I said. "If you die, does that mean I do?"

"No. You are stronger. You will be broken with grief obviously, but you will survive. Witches live longer than animals."

I would be overcome with grief if I lost this annoying crow. "I'll be careful, and I won't write anything down."

"Rest," he said. "You will be better with rest."

Phillip was in the kitchen when I got back. He was brewing tea, so something in my life was normal.

"Are you all right?" he asked. "You look like someone ran over your familiar."

"We caught the killer," I said. "You'll hear about it from Mark."

His emotions clamped down. I think he was trying to protect me. "That's good. We are safe again."

I nodded and turned to enter my bedroom.

"Tea?"

"No thanks." I opened my door and then closed out the world. The red spell bag would keep everyone away.

The boxes I'd brought from The Inner Spell were waiting for me. I reached for the one Elias and Janet found buried.

I sat on the bed and looked at it. The dirt was cleaned off and there was no sign of decay. An easy spell to preserve it, but why bother? I mean, why preserve it, why bury it?

My curiosity overcame my exhaustion. Just a peek. It probably wasn't anything important. The little voice inside my head chuckled. *Sure, someone went to the trouble of burying a box full of nothing important.*

It resisted a little at first, and then popped open. I guess Elias hadn't noticed it was just stuck, not locked.

Inside were tiny objects. I dumped them on my comforter. Fifteen of them. That couldn't be a coincidence.

These were talismans. I was sure of it. Each of these would identify someone who was there that night.

It could be adrenalin, or dopamine, but any thought of napping was chased out by this revelation.

I scanned my shelves for the books I'd borrowed from the store. Was there one that talked about talismans? Should Phillip have taught me this? Yes, but where was it on the list of priorities?

In fact, was he doing the lousy job Mrs. V thought?

Yes, I'd been here just over three weeks, and I still didn't know the basics. I couldn't rely on him for knowledge, and I would ask Mrs. V for a new mentor. He was just my landlord from now on.

My landlord and an old friend of my parents. Okay, and my part-time employer. That is one thing he did right. I could run this store on my own at any time.

Was that why he hadn't taught me about magic?

Was he planning to leave the island and needed me to run the store? No. He knew I had The Inner Spell. I was out of here as soon as I got it up and running.

I pulled the brake on that train of thought.

I'd placed a basic witchcraft book on the shelf. I needed to do some research. Tomorrow, I could talk to Mrs. V. For now, everyone on the island was on the suspect list, except D, Lilibeth, Lance, and Mrs. V.

And Mark? Not sure about him.

And Dolph? Another maybe.

43

T he next morning I followed Phillip around the store as we took inventory. It wasn't exactly exciting, but I was glad to be doing something that didn't involve chatting. Over breakfast he'd told me the news was out about Aria's murder. He hadn't outright asked me for details, but the way he told me left room for me to fill in any other information.

I kept quiet.

"That's the full process," he said as he finished putting the last of the books back on the shelves. He carried everything from the latest beach read to an esoteric medieval tome on witch identification for purification.

"Thanks, I guess I will have some inventory at The Inner Spell," I said. "Maybe I can offer space for other witches to sell their wares."

"Nice idea. Elias is starting today, is that right?" He wasn't looking at me as he asked the question, but I got the strong feeling he had another topic he wanted to raise.

"Yes," I said. "I'll be out of your hair soon. I think I'll stay in the main building, so you get your spare room back."

When I first came up with the idea, I didn't want to be so isolated by living on site. After the last few weeks of traveling around the island, I realized it wasn't so far — nothing was.

"You are always welcome here, Cossi," he said.

"That's good to hear," I said. "I need to meet with Mrs. Vestum if you have nothing else for me."

"Off you go," he said. "What I have can wait."

I tried not to think of him differently, but everything sounded like a threat. Not through my power, but just something. Given he was in the 'everyone is a suspect' group, I shouldn't be surprised. I hope I didn't get the same feeling from people like Jan or Sheena. Life was going to be very lonely if I let paranoia get to me.

Mrs. Vestum was expecting me, so I grabbed her favorite drink from Jan's and headed toward her house. I rehearsed my words as I went. I would ask for a new mentor without opening the door to her assigning herself the job. Or taking offense.

"Cossi." Mark's voice interrupted my musing and almost made me drop the drinks.

"Some notice would be nice," I said. "Do you sneak up on everyone?"

He grinned. "Not everyone is wandering around stuck in their head. Seriously, you should be alert when you're out."

He had a point, but I couldn't handle walking around like I was about to be attacked.

"Did you want something?"

"After what happened yesterday," he said, "you are going to hunt the person behind the killings, right?"

I wasn't planning on telling him about the box of talismans. He'd told us to keep our mouths shut about the secrets, so why was he asking now?

"I don't think I have a choice," I said. "If we don't stop them, we'll have nine more bodies, and possibly nine more dead murderers."

"I know. Will you let me help?"

This was the opposite of normal. He usually asked me to help him, and then kicked me off as soon as I did. Him helping me? I didn't trust him yet.

"You can't play the cop and do what we do," I said. It gave him an out.

"I'm not playing at being the cop," he said. "But I also don't have to be the cop all the time. I can help, Cossi. I know things no one else does."

"And you'll promise to let us do what's needed?"

"Unless you plan to kill someone, yes."

I looked at him as if I could tell whether he was lying. I couldn't. His emotions were tightly controlled. He could be an asset, and if the others agreed, we could all keep an eye on him until he proved himself.

"I'll think about it." I held up the drinks. "I need to get going before these get cold."

He stepped aside and let me pass. "I can keep you safe, remember that."

Two minutes later, I was in Mrs. Vestum's kitchen.

"Okay, I agree that Phillip isn't up to the job of mentor," I said. "Can you get me a new one? I'll be moving into The Inner Spell in a couple of weeks, so it would be great if Phillip didn't decide to evict me."

"He won't know it came from you," she said. "I have no extra space anyway, so we'll get him to agree to let you stay in his apartment."

Oh no. I knew exactly what she was going to say before she started.

"I'll be your mentor starting today. It's a perfect arrangement. We need to work together to find and remove the threat to Henbane."

With the festival looming, Cossi starts her business and faces another murder. Can she bring the killer to justice before the celebrations start?
Use the QR code below to grab your copy now

FREE BOOK

Claim your copy of Magic Will Out when you sign up for my newsletter and follow Cossi as she seeks answers to her past. Use the QR code to claim your copy now.

ALSO BY POPPY

For more books by Poppy Bridgeman

scan the QR code below.

ABOUT POPPY BRIDGEMAN

Hi, I'm Poppy Bridgeman, the cozy mystery alter ego of Canadian author P A Wilson. Poppy was "born" because sometimes stories need a gentler touch—with a little magic, a dash of humor, and plenty of sleuthing spirit.

As Poppy, I write the *Witch of Henbane Island* series (where witches and festivals collide with mysteries), the *EB Eats Culinary Mysteries* (a small-town diner, a determined heroine, and murder on the menu), and the *Pages & Paws Bookstore Mysteries* (a Devon bookshop, two mischievous corgis, and plenty of secrets tucked between the shelves).

When I'm not tangled in my characters' escapades, I'm happily tangled in yarn—I knit, weave, and doodle in sketchbooks between writing sessions. I also love to travel, finding inspiration for charming settings, quirky characters, and suspicious strangers wherever I go.

Home base is the Vancouver area, where I juggle writing as both Poppy and P A Wilson. Whichever name is on the cover, I'm always chasing the next story.

 X

ACKNOWLEDGMENTS

People think that the process of writing is solitary. That's not the case for me. I have help from so many people it would be hard to acknowledge everyone, but I'll give it a try.

The support and inspiration I get from my writer's groups is incalculable. The Vancouver Writers Social Group opens my mind to other ways of telling a story. The Royal City Literary Arts Society gives me the opportunity to meet and share with other writers who have more knowledge than I do. The Other 11 Months group is where I learn about getting the words on the page. And my critique group who helps me find the best parts of the story I want to tell. Thanks to all of the members of these great groups.

Last of all, but definitely a huge part of the process, my beta readers. These are the people who love stories and are willing, and more than able, to tell me if my finished story is ready for you, my readers.